MERCHANTS OF DEATH

A JAMAICAN SAGA OF DRUGS, SEX, VIOLENCE AND CORRUPTION

K. Sean Harris

Book Fetish

Cover Design: Sanya Dockery
Typeset & Book layout: Sanya Dockery

Published by: Book Fetish
www.bookfetishjamaica.com
info@bookfetishjamaica.com

Printed in the USA   ISBN 10: 976-610-760-2
                                      ISBN 13: 978-976-610-760-4

And as it is appointed unto men to die
but after this the judgement.

Hebrews 9: 27

CHAPTER 1

The lanky, fair-complexioned man strode briskly through the automatic glass door and approached the receptionist. He waited patiently as she wrapped up her telephone conversation.

"Good morning sir, sorry to have kept you waiting," she said, in a somewhat squeaky voice. "How may I help you?"

"Good morning. I'm here to see Mr. Laylor," the man replied, with what sounded like a Spanish accent.

"Do you have an appointment?" Marcia queried, as she wondered what it was about him that gave her the chills. He was well-dressed in a grey suit and a trendy striped tie; tall and fairly attractive; but his eyes...they were a very intense shade of grey, and appeared blank and lifeless; devoid of expression.

"No, I don't, just inform him that I'm an investor from Miami who was referred to him by one of his colleagues." Anthony was confident the man would see him. Based on the information he had received, Barry Laylor would never pass up an opportunity to make some money.

He watched the young lady as she spoke to her boss, smiling at him nervously. Anthony looked at her coldly, reveling in her discomfort and the knowledge that she would probably be dead in a few minutes, pending the outcome of the meeting.

"You may go in sir," she announced, "second door on the right."

Marcia watched as he nodded and strode purposefully down the hall, relieved to be rid of his blank, expressionless gaze. Weird man, she thought, as she went back to her paperwork.

Anthony felt the familiar rush of adrenaline course through his veins as he neared his target. He felt like God. Some men were born to be doctors, others athletes; Anthony Garcia was a natural born killer. The son of a Jamaican fisherman and a Cuban prostitute, his first victim had been an older boy who constantly teased him about his unusual eyes and quiet demeanor. Anthony had followed the boy into the trash-infested alley behind the illegal gambling den and slit his throat as he relieved himself. He had felt a surge of power run through his fifteen year old body as he watched Pedro writhe on the grimy street in agony; urine and blood flowing from his soon to be lifeless body. After that episode, it became common knowledge on the streets of Havana that the quiet chico with the grey eyes was not one to be fucked with.

Anthony rapped on the thick pine door firmly.

"Come in," came a gruff voice from inside. Anthony stepped into the plush office and closed the door behind him.

"Have a seat," Barry Laylor offered, staring at his unexpected guest. "So," he began, reclining in his swivel chair and clasping his hands around his generous stomach, "which of my colleagues referred me to you?"

Anthony stared coldly at the obese man opposite him.

"Pablo Hernandez."

Laylor's eyes popped open wide in surprise. He had been laundering drug money for Hernandez and his associates for several months now. It had been great at first and he was richly compensated for his services, but things were different now. The Jamaican police had recently enlisted the help of their British counterparts to aid them in curbing the violence that currently had the island in a vice grip; and at the top of the list were drug dealers and money laundering. Paying off or evading the Jamaican police was one thing, but cops from Scotland Yard was a whole different ballgame; it was time to get out while the going was good. Pablo Hernandez hadn't taken the news well. Called him a coward, and a hijo de puta, which he later learnt meant son of a bitch. Ah boy, the nerve of that fucking criminal! You lie down with dog, you must catch fleas, Laylor thought bitterly.

"So why are you here?" Laylor demanded, suddenly getting very irate. "Yuh think say mi ah go jail so that him can stay ah Cuba and get richer? You must be rass mad!"

Anthony was unimpressed by the outburst.

"So you refuse to co-operate?" he asked calmly.

"Get out of my office!" Laylor exploded, his double chin bobbing as his fleshy face shook with anger. "Nuh puss eye bwoy from Cuba can't come pon my turf and strong arm mi! You go back to Hernandez and tell him that no means no, the party over!"

Anthony rose suddenly and squeezed off three quick shots, the bullets grotesquely distorting Barry's fat face upon impact, the sound muffled by the silencer attached to the slender but powerful handgun. Anthony shot him again for good measure, peeved at being referred to as a 'puss eye bwoy'; he was very sensitive about his eyes. He watched blankly as copious amounts of blood seeped from the dead man's head onto the thick beige carpet. Anthony straightened his tie and stepped out of the expansive office, closing the door softly behind him.

That was quick, Marcia thought as she looked up to see the man re-enter the lobby. Anthony walked towards her desk, his left hand dangling slightly behind his leg, concealing the weapon it held.

"Anything else I can assist you with?" she asked pleasantly, sounding forced to her own ears, but damn it, good looking or not, something was off about him.

"Yes," Anthony replied and casually raised his gun, holding it level with her oval face. Marcia felt moisture seep down her thighs as her bladder emptied itself of the two cups of coffee she had consumed earlier. She stared stupidly at the gun, her mouth open wide in a silent scream. The bullet entered her brain via her left eye, killing her instantly.

Anthony placed the gun inside his jacket and checked the time on his Movado; it was 9:30. I wonder what I should have for breakfast he pondered as he exited the building and walked to the grey, tinted Range Rover, one of several luxury vehicles his boss owned in Jamaica. As he drove towards the gate, he briefly contemplated killing the security guard, but decided against it as the man had not seen his face. He tooted his horn instead and the guard waved as he drove into the light traffic streaming down Constant Spring Road. Anthony drove for ten minutes and then turned onto Hope Road, deciding to have a nice Jamaican breakfast of ackee & saltfish at one of the restaurants on Kingston's hip strip. He would report to Hernandez after he had eaten.

Terri Miller was in her sleek, red Mazda Miata heading to a meeting with the Assistant Police Commissioner when the news came on the radio: *The bodies of prominent Kingston businessman, Barry Laylor and his secretary were found at his office on Constant Spring Road this morning by his lawyer who made the gruesome find when he went there for a 9:45 meeting with his client. Details are...*Oh my god, Terri thought as her cell phone rang. It was the Assistant Commissioner.

"Corporal Miller, have you heard about the killings?" He asked in a voice raspy from too many cigarettes and over proof rum. Assistant Commissioner Mayweather was not known for his good manners.

"Good morning sir, I just heard it on the news," Terri replied.

"I'm putting off our meeting until six this evening, go to the crime scene immediately and ensure that everything is properly secured. A couple officers are already there and the vultures are circling," He instructed, hanging up without waiting for a response.

Vultures...Mayweather hated the press with a passion, but then, he didn't like anything or anyone, Terri mused, as she remembered the time he had come on to her in her rookie year. She had politely but firmly declined his clumsy invitation to 'knock back a few rounds' at his apartment. As if! The man was so repulsive. He had never forgiven her for the rebuff and made things difficult for her whenever the opportunity presented itself. Terri turned onto to Waterloo Road and increased her speed, hoping those bumbling idiots she had as co-workers hadn't tampered with the crime scene. So many unsolved cases were due to crime scenes not being properly processed. What a way to start the day, Terri thought, whipping the car through traffic, at least the job is never boring.

Terri Miller was an enigma in the Jamaica Police Force. The only daughter of a tenured professor and a dermatologist, she could have been anything she wanted but inexplicably chose one of the most hazardous jobs one could undertake in Jamaica — becoming a cop.

Armed with youth — she was twenty-four at the time, a second degree in Forensic Psychology and a flair for danger; she entered the force at the level of Inspector. She was given a hard time at first, most of her peers and superiors felt intimidated by her educated, privileged background and her stunning good looks. She had slowly won most of them over with her above-average intelligence, down to earth attitude and fearlessness on the job. In four short years, she had risen to the rank of Detective Corporal, and was widely acknowledged as the top investigator in the country.

Terri had gained national prominence after solving the brutal triple homicide that had rocked the nation three years ago. Seeing the killers bought to justice had done a lot for the psyche of a people gripped with fear and disgust at the new breed of ruthless criminals roaming the streets.

Across town, at the Jonboo Restaurant, Anthony was stuffing his face with ackee & saltfish and soft green boiled bananas. He watched the television mounted on the wall a couple feet away through his reddish-tint Gucci sunglasses. He stopped eating and paid rapt attention when a news update came on, and the press swarmed a lovely, well-dressed young woman, asking her questions about the brutal murder. She declined comment as she navigated her way through the throng of reporters and went through the gate, which was now manned by several grim looking police officers. *Caliente*, Anthony thought, dabbing his lips with a napkin. He had heard about the popular detective but had no idea she was so young and beautiful. He felt a stirring in his loins. A reporter was now saying that they would have further updates as the day progresses. Anthony sipped his coffee and took out his cell phone to update his boss.

Pablo Hernandez was at his luxurious villa in Havana, Cuba, lying on his stomach, naked, getting a massage when the red phone rang. Only two people had this number; his lawyer and Anthony, his trusted hit man whom he thought of as a son. He waved away the nubile masseuse and answered immediately.

"Hola," he said, sitting up and lighting a cigar.

"Padre, it's me," Anthony said. "He's dead. The fool refused to budge."

"Si, no problemo," Hernandez replied, "He was getting on my nerves anyway, with his fucking whining about the cops. I despise cowards. My lawyer has a new contact lined up; he's a manager at a merchant bank. He'll wash our money in Jamaica from now on."

"Si padre," Anthony said, adding, "The cops are all over the scene as we speak."

"Fuck 'em," Hernandez chuckled, "I know you don't leave witnesses and besides, there's no record of you even being in the country, so let them investigate. Before the week is out, they'll have a lot more investigating to do....I plan to step up my presence on the island and that means taking care of some of those so-called dons."

"What time are you coming in tomorrow?" Anthony asked, as he signaled for the waitress to bring the bill.

"Not sure yet, depends on whether I use the plane or the yacht," He replied, puffing on his Cuban cigar. "I'll call you and let you know."

"Ok Padre, adios," Anthony said as he hung up the phone. He paid his bill, leaving a huge tip for the waitress and stepped out into the bright, almost midday sunshine. He had a couple of hours to kill before he met with a man known only as Wild Apache. He controlled the underworld of East Kingston and Hernandez wanted him to have a preliminary meeting today; in the upcoming months, he will need allies to take control of the Jamaican drug game and Wild Apache would be a good man to have on the team. Anthony had sent a message to him and he agreed to meet in the afternoon at his base in the ghetto of Rockfort. Anthony checked his watch and decided to visit his favourite escort service to kill some time; seeing that sexy cop had made him horny.

CHAPTER 2

Terri issued instructions to the officers on the scene and an hour later when all the evidence had been collected, she ordered the bodies removed so that an autopsy could be done. As she waited for them to bring in the security guard who was on duty that morning, she wondered what the hell Laylor had gotten himself mixed up in. It was obviously a hit, professionally done. Laylor's licensed firearm had been in his waist when he got shot. She browsed through his cell phone and realized the phonebook was locked. Terri made a mental note to obtain his phone records from his network provider. She hoped the guard would have some useful information as the perpetrator had not left any clues behind, except for his shell casings.

"Corporal Miller, here is the guard," the young officer with the funny shaped nose said, poking his head in the office.

"Send him in," she replied, folding her arms around her ample bosom.

"How are you, I'm Inspector Miller," she said to him pleasantly, extending her hand.

The security guard shook it delightedly, grinning as he told her he knew who she was, having seen her on television countless times.

Terri subtly extricated her hand from the man's callous, sweaty palms.

"Do you keep a log book of the vehicles that enter the premises on a daily basis?" Terri asked, not in the least bothered by the lustful way in which the guard was staring at her.

"No ma'am," He replied, adding, "But ah remember that only four vehicles come in this morning before dem find the bodies."

"Ok, good," Terri said, "Go on..."

"Missa Laylor black van, Miss Marcia little car, a SUV and the lawyer benz," the guard proudly related, happy to be helping out, maybe he would get mentioned in the news.

"Describe the SUV."

"Well, is a new one and it look really expensive. It name something and nedda Rover."

"Ok...did you happen to see the occupant or occupants?"

"De who?" the guard asked, looking bewildered.

"The driver and or passengers," Terri explained patiently.

"Ohhh! Mi never really see him good, but it was a man and it look like ah him alone did in there."

"Approximately what time did this vehicle enter the premises and roughly how long did it stay?"

"Ummm, it come in bout after nine, and it never stay long...bout fifteen minutes or so."

"Thank you very much sir. Call me anytime if you remember anything further," Terri said as she gave him an embossed business card and ushered him out the door.

She closed the door and stood there, looking out the large window behind Layor's desk, processing the information she got from the guard. Hmmm, my killer has expensive tastes she mused, looking at the shrubs waving in the hot air. She wished he had gotten a good look at the driver but at least she had something to go on.

Forty-five minutes later, Terri was at her mother's office, knowing she would want to gossip about the murder. She had been acquaintances with Laylor's first wife, when she used to be on the board of the High School committee of which she was the president, and Barry Laylor had been a prominent, high-profile businessman. Terri had picked up two boxes of Chinese takeout and the elder Mrs. Miller was pleasantly surprised to see her daughter. They lunched, and Terri filled her in as best she could without disclosing confidential information.

At this time, Anthony was getting ready to have a second go with the young, voluptuous girl he had selected at the upscale, discreet escort service. She was good, and didn't talk much, which pleased him greatly. Anthony gripped her silky hair as she pleasured him with her knowledgeable mouth. Anthony closed his grey eyes and thought of Detective Miller as his swollen member throbbed and pulsed deeply in the girl's mouth. Ten minutes later after she had drunk all he had to offer, he gave her a nice tip and called Wild Apache, informing him that he would be there in an hour.

Anthony puffed on a Cuban cigar and reminisced on the day he had met Pablo Hernandez as he headed towards his rendezvous. It had been about three days after he had killed Pedro, when two men had approached him at the seedy gambling den where he ran errands for the owner, telling him Pablo Hernandez wanted to see him. He had been surprised but not scared, to learn that one of the most notorious crime lords in Cuba wanted to see him. They had driven to the villa in silence and the goons instructed him to go around to the swimming pool where the boss was waiting. Hernandez was sitting in a lounge chair at the poolside, sipping an orange coloured drink from a large glass; a tall, exotic looking woman in a white two-piece bathing suit massaging his shoulders.

He had walked over to him, stopped at a respectful distance and waited for the gangster to speak. Hernandez had looked at him for a long time and then suddenly asked, "Why did you kill him?"

"Because he deserved it," Anthony had replied simply.

Hernandez had laughed boisterously, instantly liking the quiet boy with the deadly looking grey eyes. That had been twelve years ago. Since that time, Anthony's unwavering loyalty, natural good looks and his chilling ability to take a life without blinking, had made him the eyes and ears of the powerful gangster. Anthony had learnt a lot from him. Pablo had encouraged him to read and taught him a lot about life. Pablo was truly the father he never had.

Anthony reached the entrance to the Rockfort community and pulled over to the side of the road as per Wild Apache's instructions. Thirty seconds passed and a short, stocky man dressed in army fatigues approached the vehicle and knocked on the window on the passenger side. Anthony released the locks and the guy climbed into the vehicle, bringing with him a pungent odor of marijuana and sweat.

"Yes, King," the man offered by way of greeting.

Anthony nodded in response and they drove off up the narrow lane leading into the heart of the volatile inner-city community. Anthony heard the roar of powerful engines and noticed that two high powered motorbikes were behind them. They drove in silence until the man remarked, "So mi hear say the I is a big time hitman."

Anthony stared impassively ahead, mulling if he should kill the man right here and now. He obviously didn't know how to conduct himself. That was an inexcusable lapse of judgement. He decided against it, but would definitely see to it at a later date.

"Yuh not much of a talker eh?" He said gruffly, when he realized that Anthony did not intend to respond. Anthony ignored him and glanced at his surroundings as he drove. The community was squalid; the sides of the road were filled with trash and debris, little kids ran up and down the streets playing, dirty and barefooted, blissfully oblivious to the condition of their surroundings; young, dangerous looking men sat in groups on corners, looking coldly at the luxurious vehicle as it drove by; while voluptuous women and young girls in skimpy outfits walked around talking and laughing loudly.

"Right here so," the man said, as they reached the largest house in the community at the end of the dead end street.

Anthony stopped the Range Rover and alighted from the vehicle. He nodded at the two men on the motorbikes and followed his garrulous guide into the spacious yard. They walked along the side of the house and went around to the backyard where there were approximately twelve men standing with various high powered weapons. Anthony walked straight towards the only man that was sitting. The diminutive man with the straggly Indian hair slouching on the well-worn patio chair smoking a spliff was obviously the infamous Wild Apache. He was shirtless and had a chrome revolver tucked in his waist.

"Greetings, Wild Apache," Anthony said, as he came to a stop directly in front of him.

"Yes, King," Wild Apache replied in a quiet voice. "Mek we go inside go talk business."

Anthony followed him through the back door and into a sort of den where Wild Apache offered him a beer. Anthony accepted. They talked shop for over an hour, Anthony laying out the blueprint Hernandez had for stepping up his operations in Jamaica. Hernandez would provide the financing and other resources, and Wild Apache would provide the soldiers and the local underworld connections. Hernandez would be the top dog with the final say in all operations.

Wild Apache agreed to the terms, thinking to himself that he would dispose of the Cuban after things were up and running. He was a don and nuh pussyhole from Cuba nah come yah and order him around. But he could play nice 'till the money start run. As they shook hands, Anthony thought inwardly that he would kill the smelly Indian as soon as he had outlived his usefulness.

"Alright, so we'll be in touch," Anthony said as he rose to leave. "By the way, the guy you sent to meet me talks too much. Asks too many questions."

"Ah mi cousin man," Wild Apache responded, "Nuh watch nutten. Everything cool."

Anthony looked at him for a moment and then stepped out into the yard. The cousin in question escorted him out to his vehicle. This time he was silent on the ride back out of Rockfort. Anthony thanked God for small mercies.

Terri felt tired after exiting police headquarters. After lunch with her mom, she had followed up some leads on three cases she was working on, including the double murder that morning. Then at six she had to endure the unpleasant task of briefing Asst. Commissioner Mayweather for the better part of an hour, though she was most pleased with herself for remaining stoic when he stood up to flaunt his erection. She was determined not to let him get to her. Terri opened her car and got in, wishing she had a strong pair of knowledgeable hands waiting at home to give her a massage. Terri appraised her life as she exited the premises and started the forty-five minute journey to her lovely two-bedroom apartment in Stony Hill. She was twenty-seven, promising career, gorgeous, yet single. Most men seemed to be intimidated by her; and the few who weren't acted as if they're in awe of her, like she's some kind of trophy and she really hated that. Her last boyfriend, Douglas, had left her three months ago and was now living in New York with a white woman. Only a white woman would tolerate your insecure, trifling ass Terri had told him when he had informed her of his decision. He had said some really nasty things to her that night but she hadn't been hurt as she had known that the breakup was inevitable. Though he had relished the perceived status that came from dating her, Douglas had always felt intimidated by her. Always the realist, she had expected it to last six months. It lasted eight. She had only dated him because the loneliness had been eating at her and she had needed some sex badly. At least he hadn't been too bad at that, especially oral. He had thoroughly enjoyed going down on her. Terri sighed as she stopped at the gas station to fill up her tank, it was at halfway mark and she didn't like it to dip below that. She absently played with hair as she watched the attendant pump the gas, thinking that the car wasn't the only thing that needed filling.

Assistant Commissioner Claude Mayweather sat at his untidy desk mulling over the information that he had received from Cpl. Miller. She knew the make of the vehicle the killer drove, the type of weapon fired and by Monday she would have the phone records for Layor's cell phone and land lines. She was a balls-buster but the bitch was efficient he mused as he took a flask of rum out of his desk drawer. He had endured a turgid erection for the duration of the meeting. To his annoyance, the bitch hadn't even flinched when he stood up pretending to pace the room so that she could see his erection. If only the wife could get it up like that Mayweather thought ruefully as he took a swig of the rum. The phone on his desk rang loudly, and he answered after the fourth ring when he remembered that Sonia, his secretary, had already gone home for the evening.

"Hello," he said gruffly.

"Honey, what time are you coming home?" Elaine, his wife of twelve years asked him pleasantly.

"When I get there!" Mayweather growled and slammed down the phone.

Elaine stood in their comfortable living room, with the phone still by her ear, tears streaming down her fleshy cheeks, wondering why her husband seemed to hate her.

After leaving Rockfort, Anthony had driven up to the mansion in Stony Hill, where members of the organization stayed whenever they were in Jamaica. It was a large, airy two-storey house, comprising of eight bedrooms, four bathrooms, a large kitchen and a swimming pool at the back. Hernandez had purchased the house through his Jamaican lawyer over a year ago. The lawyer sent up his own personal house-keeper to ready the house and purchase groceries whenever he was advised that the house would be occupied. Anthony had been in Jamaica for two days now. He had arrived on one of Hernandez's small planes that was primarily used for drug smuggling, and the lawyer, a jet black complexioned man by the name of Gavin Wilkinson, had picked him up from the private airstrip. The morning after he had arrived in the island, he had been in the kitchen, nude, when Mavis, the helper, had come by to finish up some cleaning. She had blushed furiously at his nakedness, while he coolly told her good morning and continued to drink his orange juice. He had declined her offer of breakfast and had left shortly after to meet with Barry Laylor.

Now groggy from his late afternoon nap, Anthony decided to take a shower and head out to New Kingston for some dinner and entertainment.

Terri headed straight for the bathroom when she got home. She lit her candles, prepared a bubble bath and soaked away the day in the tub, while listening to the smooth sounds of Garnett Silk, one of her favourite Reggae singers. Forty five minutes later, feeling refreshed and wrapped in a plush white towel, she called her close friend Anna to see what she was up to.

"Hello," Anna said chirpily, answering on the second ring.

"Hey girl, it's me," Terri said, "What are you up to?"

"Hi Terri! I was planning to call you tonight," She said enthusiastically, adding, "We're going on the road tonight; we haven't hung out in ages."

"I know...I've just been really busy, but I'm game tonight. I really need to unwind," Terri replied, looking at the breathtaking view of the city from her patio.

"What you really need is some good dick!" Anna said, laughing.

"I won't argue that one," Terri agreed, chuckling.

"Ok, let's meet at Cobbler Lounge; tonight they have Spanish cuisine and Latin music."

"Sounds good; I'll see you at about nine," Terri said and hung up the phone. Anna was something else, Terri mused fondly. She loved Anna like a sister though they were as different as night and day. They had met in high school and whereas Terri had been athletic and studious, Anna was more into boys and fashion and partying. Somewhere along the line they discovered that they really liked each other and had been close ever since. After high school, Terri went to University on a scholarship while Anna was discovered by a modeling agency and went on to become a fairly successful runway model. Terri was the prettier of the two, but Anna was taller and more exotic looking. Anna changed men as often as she changed her underwear, and was forever entertaining Terri with her 'sexcapades'. She was currently seeing one of the stars on the national football team and confided to Terri that the man was hung like a horse. Terri loved sex and was a very passionate woman but she just couldn't bring herself to sleep around indiscriminately. Terri checked the time, and rummaged through her closet for something to wear. It would take her at least forty minutes to get to New Kingston so she had best get cracking.

CHAPTER 3

Anthony pulled into the semi-crowded parking lot at the Cobbler Lounge a few minutes before nine. He had called Gavin to ask him where he could get authentic Spanish food in Kingston and was told this was the spot for all things Spanish on a Friday night. Anthony exited the vehicle and took in his surroundings as he straightened his white blazer. Two pretty young women strutted past him and the taller of the two smiled at him invitingly as they passed. Maybe later, Anthony mused as he closed the door and activated the alarm. He had driven the BMW convertible instead of the Range Rover. Assistant Commissioner Mayweather had called him a couple hours ago to inform him of the status of the investigation and to voice his annoyance at not being told of the hit. Anthony had curtly told him that his job was to provide them with information, not the other way around. The police were on the lookout for a late model Range Rover so he had parked it inside the spacious garage at the mansion. I should have killed the security guard, Anthony thought, planning to rectify that tomorrow. His cell phone rang as he approached the lounge. It was Hernandez.

"Tony, did you meet with the guy?" Hernandez enquired, always one to get business out of the way before any small talk.

"Yeah," Anthony replied, "Everything is on stream."

"Good, good…I'll be coming in on the yacht tomorrow about midday. Meet me at the harbour in Port Royal and bring Gavin," Hernandez instructed.

"Roger that padre," Anthony replied, feeling his heartbeat accelerate a bit as he watched a familiar looking woman exit a red sports car. It was that gorgeous female cop.

"So what are you doing tonight?" Hernandez asked, as he counted the stacks of US currency on the table in front of him. One of his couriers had just returned from a drug run and he was making sure the money was right.

"I'm at this lounge Gavin told me about, they have Spanish food and music here tonight," Anthony told him; his eyes glued to Terri as she glanced at him before entering the lounge.

"Have fun, see you tomorrow," Hernandez said and terminated the call.

Anthony pushed the swing doors and went inside. The host met him at the door and escorted him to a table. Salsa music blared through the surround speakers and a few couples were on the small dance floor having fun; some people were milling around, drinking, smoking and chatting in groups; while others were seated at the tables digging into various Spanish dishes. The crowd was a good mix of young to middle-aged affluent looking people; a nice upscale ambience. Anthony looked at the menu and ordered paella along with a bottle of vino roja. Having placed his order, Anthony casually looked around to see if he could find the cop. He spotted her about four tables away. She was seated with her back to him, deep in conversation with an exotic looking woman with short spiky hair.

Terri laughed as she listened to Anna's latest sexual episode. Apparently her football boyfriend was away in the US representing Jamaica in the Gold Cup tournament which was being held in Florida. Unable to hold out until he returned, she had given a business executive a chance to sample the goods but he had turned out to be a one minute man. Literally.

"Lots of cute men in here tonight Terri," Anna said as she sexily pulled on a cigarette. "There's an immaculately dressed one sitting a couple tables away behind you and he's alone girl."

Terri discreetly turned her head and looked. The man was staring at her. She held his gaze for a couple seconds before turning back around.

"I saw him outside when I was coming in, he is cute...has the most unusual grey eyes I've ever seen," Terri told Anna as the waiter arrived with their order.

"I just love a man who knows how to dress," Anna said as she dug into her fritatas.

"I'm trying to get Raymond to start putting a little more effort in his dressing but he's so damn stubborn! If his cock wasn't so big I would've kicked him to the curb a long time ago."

Terri chuckled and sipped her wine; wondering if 'Mr. Grey Eyes' was still staring at her. Anthony watched as various people went over to their table to say hi, quite the celebrity he mused as the pretty young woman who had smiled at him in the parking lot came to sit in front of him.

"Hi handsome, I'm Dana," she purred, offering her hand.

"Tony," He replied coolly, as he shook her hand.

"Would you like some company?" she asked, looking directly in his eyes.

"I would definitely like your company, but unfortunately I'm waiting for someone," Anthony lied smoothly. "Maybe some other time?"

"Oooh I just love your accent," Dana cooed, "Here's my number. Call me...anytime."

"Will do," Anthony replied, slipping the number in the pocket of his blazer. He looked over at Terri's table and sipped his wine.

"Look at that little tramp trying to steal your man Terri," Anna joked, as they looked at the girl rising from the table and looking at Anthony flirtatiously.

As Terri looked around she found herself meeting his gaze for the third time that night. She felt a sudden urge to pee.

"I'm going to the ladies room," Terri said, "Be right back."

She had to pass Anthony's table to get to the bathroom and was a bit annoyed with herself at the bubbles she was feeling in her stomach. Stop acting like a damn schoolgirl Terri! She chided herself inwardly. She avoided looking at him as she passed his table. Five minutes later, on her way back to her table, Anthony gently held on to her hand as she passed by. She stopped and faced him.

"Do you make a habit of grabbing women you don't know?" Terri asked him softly, making no attempt to remove her hand.

"Please, join me," Anthony replied, gesturing to the seat in front of him. "Your friend won't mind," He added, as Terri opened her mouth to protest.

Terri glanced over at her table. Anna smiled and raised her glass to her, and gestured for her to stay over there. Terri sighed and sat down.

"I'm Anthony," He said to her as he gestured for the waiter to bring him another glass.

"I'm Terri, Terri Miller," she replied, as he poured her a glass of red wine.

"You are without a doubt the most beautiful woman I've ever seen," Anthony said, giving her a piercing look she could not read.

"Thank you," Terri said softly. She was used to such declarations from men but was warmed by his compliment. Terri looked at him appraisingly over her wine glass. He was a handsome man, strong jaw line, prominent cheek bones, confident and nattily attired. And those eyes...they had her mesmerized. But what attracted her to him most, was the air of danger that seemed to emanate from him. Terri sensed that beneath that polished, quiet demeanor was a lot more lurking than met the eye.

"You're Hispanic." A statement.

"Yes, I'm half Cuban, half Jamaican," Anthony replied easily, adding, "I reside in Cuba but I'm frequently in Jamaica."

"What do you do, if you don't mind me asking," Terri said coyly, toying with her wine glass.

"I work with my uncle who has various business interests both here and in Cuba." Anthony reached over and lightly caressed her hands. "Enough about me," he said, looking deeply in her eyes, "tell me about Terri."

Terri chuckled inwardly at his changing of the subject, something to hide maybe? "Not much to tell really. I'm a Police Officer, single and childless. My job is very demanding and takes up a lot of my time and energy. Tonight is the first time I've been out in weeks."

"Let's dance," Anthony suggested, rising from his seat and offering her his hand. Terri, having taken salsa lessons over two years ago, wondered if she would remember all the moves, but not one to back down from a challenge, she accepted his invitation. He took her hand

and led her to the small dance floor. The rust quickly wore off as Terri lost herself in the infectious music. She felt sexy and utterly feminine as Anthony twirled, spun and lifted her all over the dance floor; he was an excellent dancer. He held her close as the beat slowed down, and she could feel that he was aroused. He pressed his body against hers, gazing down at her with a predatory look in his eyes. She felt hot all over. Anthony suddenly broke the embrace and led her from the dance floor. As he signaled for the cheque, Terri looked around for Anna; she was nowhere to be seen. Probably off with some guy Terri thought, watching Anthony as he paid the bill by cash and gave the waiter a huge tip. I can't do this Terri thought, as she exited the lounge with Anthony, no way I'm sleeping with him tonight, no matter what my body...

"Terri...," Anthony said breaking in her thoughts, "I need to be inside you." They were now standing in the parking lot.

"Anthony...I just met..." Anthony crushed her to him and invaded her mouth with his tongue, cutting her off in mid sentence. Terri hesitated at first, then returned his kiss ardently and slid her hand inside his blazer. She broke the kiss suddenly, peering up into his face. "Do you have a permit to carry that weapon Anthony?" she asked him seriously, her face flush from her uncharacteristic lustful behaviour.

Anthony slid her other hand to the bulge in his slacks. "I have a permit for both of them," he said, nibbling on her lips gently.

"Anthony...stop...we're in public," Terri breathed, she was extremely wet.

"Your place or mine?" Anthony asked; his grey eyes alive with lust.

Terri inhaled the cool night air deeply and cleared her head. Anthony was gazing at her confidently. A bit too confidently, Terri thought. She eased out of his arms.

"Anthony, I can't sleep with you. I don't even know you," Terri said softly, but firmly.

"Why are you fighting it?" He ran his fingers lightly along her jaw line. "Look me in the eyes and tell me you don't want me."

Terri sighed. "I'm amazed at how attracted I am to you," she admitted, "but I can't just hop into bed with you like that. I'm an old fashioned girl Tony."

Anthony chuckled ruefully. "Ok Ms. Miller, we'll do it your way. Here's my number."

They exchanged numbers and Anthony hugged her tightly, wanting her to feel his erection. He watched as Terri waved and entered her car. She pulled out of her parking spot and stopped at his feet. She put her window down.

"Don't do anything I wouldn't do," she said, smiling.

"I'll call you to make sure you got home safe," Anthony said, already contemplating his next move. He needed to do something with his erection. He hadn't had blue balls since he was sixteen, and he wasn't planning on starting again tonight.

"Bye Anthony," Terri said and drove off. Anthony watched the car quickly disappear. She's got a heavy foot, he mused as he fished out the napkin with the girl's number from his pocket. Anthony walked over to his car and got in as he waited for the girl to answer the phone. She answered on the fifth ring.

"Hello," she said, sounding a bit tipsy.

"Dana, it's Anthony; we met a little while ago," Anthony said as he started the car and put the top down.

"Ah, Mr. Handsome," Dana said; immediately recognizing his voice. "What's up?"

"Where are you?" Anthony asked.

"I'm in the bathroom at the lounge," she replied, adding, "What happened to the woman I saw you leave with?"

"I'm outside in the parking lot in a metallic blue convertible, come outside in three minutes," Anthony said arrogantly, ignoring her question.

"I'm on my way," she purred, his arrogance and confidence turning her on immensely. The car sounded hot too.

Anthony turned on the radio and settled on a station playing slow reggae jams. He turned it up a bit. He watched her as she stepped out into the parking lot. She spotted him immediately and approached the car with a twitch in her curvy hips. Dana slid in the car gracefully.

"Nice car," she commented, reclining in the plush leather seat.

"Thanks," Anthony replied, and drove out as onlookers gawked at the posh BMW. It was the latest 3 series and currently the only one in the island. Anthony looked like a movie star. They drove in silence for the next fifteen minutes as Anthony whipped through the light traffic at high speed. Anthony glanced over at her full, cherry painted lips and asked her if she had ever given head in a convertible with the top down going a hundred and thirty kilometers per hour. She licked her lips in response and warned him that she doubted he'd be able to control the car once her lips got a hold of him. Anthony chuckled and used one hand to free his erection. She released her seat belt and slowly took his dick in her mouth. Anthony moaned softly and increased his speed as she got into a steady rhythm. Her warm mouth felt delicious as the cool air whipped his face. He dangerously ran a red light at an intersection as he pushed the high performance luxury vehicle to dangerous speeds. He erupted in her mouth as the car began the ascent to Stony Hill. He trembled but that was his only visible reaction, the car never slowed. Dana rose and daintily wiped the corners of her pert mouth with a piece of tissue from her small handbag.

"That was a nice appetizer," Anthony remarked, checking the time and reminding himself to call Terri before she fell asleep.

They pulled into the driveway of the mansion ten minutes later. Dana looked around at the spacious manicured lawn, the large, tasteful mansion and thought to herself that this guy must be loaded. They went into the house and Anthony led the way to the kitchen where he extracted a bottle of white wine from the refrigerator. He opened the bottle and poured a glass for Dana. She took a sip and placed it on the counter in the middle of the kitchen. She then climbed onto the counter and began to take off her clothes with a sensuous striptease. Anthony put a finger to his lips, indicating for her to be quiet and dialed Terri's number on his cell phone. He watched as she slid her top off, exposing her firm, mouthwatering breasts. Terri answered on the second ring.

"Hi Anthony," Terri breathed, "I thought you had broken your promise to call."

"I couldn't forget you if I tried," He replied, looking at Dana as she slowly slipped off her skirt. She wasn't wearing any underwear. Her genitalia gaped at him.

"Are you in bed?" Anthony asked; his dick fully erect as Dana stood with her legs wide apart, caressing her body slowly and licking her lips suggestively.

"Yep, I'm all tucked in. Are you home yet?" She asked.

"Yeah, just got in, I'm going to take a shower and hit the sack. I'll talk to you soon."

"Ok, sleep tight," Terri replied and hung up; a bit disappointed that he didn't want to stay longer on the phone. She was far from sleepy.

Anthony shrugged off his blazer and Dana's eyes opened wide when she saw the handgun hanging under his armpit in a holster. She had seen guns up close before, her dad had a licensed revolver and a rifle that he used to hunt birds but she had never seen a handgun like the one Anthony had, except in the movies. Anthony watched her as he took off the rest of his clothes. When he was through he took a swig from the wine bottle and gestured for her to get down from the counter. She stepped down and he kissed her breasts sensuously, twirling her erect nipples in his mouth. Dana moaned and cupped his head, momentarily forgetting her discomfort about his gun. After massaging her vulva and nibbling on her breasts and neck, Anthony slipped on a condom and bent her over the kitchen counter. He entered her from behind, driving his dick into her as hard as he could. She implored him to fuck her harder. A real freak, Anthony mused, as he slapped her heart-shaped ass viciously while he ravaged her. Thirty minutes later, spent and sweaty, Anthony gathered his clothes along with his gun and told her to call a cab. When he saw the look of incredulity on her face, he told her not to worry, he would pay for it. Dana was about to curse him when she noticed how cold his grey eyes had become. She swallowed her retort and got dressed. Fucking bastard she fumed, as she sat in the couch waiting for the cab to show up. Anthony came strolling in the living room, wearing a pair of silk boxers and came over to her.

He extended a thousand dollar bill. "This should cover the taxi fare," he said.

"I don't need your money," Dana snapped, "I have enough."

Anthony gave her a vicious slap across her face. "Take the money bitch, and watch your tone."

Dana, in a state of shock, took the money as she clutched her jaw, which stung mightily from the force of his slap.

A horn beeped outside indicating the taxi had arrived. Dana hurriedly walked by him as he opened the door.

"Take care, pretty girl, if you're lucky I might give you a call one of these days," Anthony said as she stepped outside.

Dana shuddered and hurried into the cab, slamming the door behind her. Cursing herself for having gotten into this mess, she wondered what she would tell her boyfriend about her face, which knowing her skin, would be puffy and swollen by the time she got home.

Assistant Police Commissioner Mayweather arrived home at two in the morning. After leaving the office a little after seven, he had rounded up a few of his drinking buddies and they met at a restaurant for dinner, after which they descended on the newest strip club in Kingston, and made a spectacle of themselves for the next four hours. His wife, though awake, didn't stir when he entered the bedroom. She watched as he stripped down to his birthday suit in the semi-dark room. He was fully erect and reeked of alcohol. She wrinkled her nose when he climbed onto the bed and threw the covers off her. He flipped her towards him roughly, and administered a hard slap to the side of her head when she tried to resist his advances. Elaine cried out as her husband pushed her white cotton nightdress up around her waist and ripped her underwear from her body. He punched her in the ribs when she attempted to close her legs, and entered her dry vagina with a brutal thrust. Ignoring her cries, Mayweather rode his wife roughly, wishing that it was Cpl. Miller that was spread-eagled in pain beneath him. He climaxed twenty minutes later, rolled off his wife and promptly fell asleep. Elaine lay there bloody and sore, sobbing in pain and humiliation as she wondered if she would ever find the courage to leave the bastard. She then staggered out of bed and walked gingerly to the bathroom to clean herself.

CHAPTER 4

nthony woke up at eight-thirty the next morning. He promptly
got out of bed, stretched his six foot two frame and did a
quick twenty minute workout of crunches and push-ups. He
retrieved his cell phone and dialed Assistant Commissioner
Mayweather's home number. His wife answered the phone.

"Hello, good morning," she said, in a voice laced with fatigue.

"Hi, is Claude in?" Anthony asked.

"Yes but he's sleeping," she advised.

"Wake him up, it's extremely urgent I speak with him," Anthony
replied firmly.

Elaine Mayweather was silent for a few seconds and then she
sighed and told him to hold on. A grumpy, groggy Mayweather came
over the line a minute later.

"Yeah," he intoned gruffly.

"Wake your ass up Claude, I need the address and phone number
of that security guard," Anthony informed him without preamble.

"I don't have that information here at home Garcia," he replied,
seething inwardly at being spoken to in such a disrespectful manner.

"Well wherever it is, get it and call me in forty-five minutes,"
Anthony advised and hung up the phone. Mayweather slammed the
cordless phone into the wall in anger. God I hate that bastard, he
fumed as he got up to go into the bathroom. They paid him well for
his services but he hated the Spanish bastards with a passion. Now
that his bank accounts were sufficiently swollen, he would terminate
them with his special unit when the opportunity presented itself. His

mood improved rapidly as he turned on the shower. Yes, he would have every last one of them killed. Hell, he might even pull the trigger himself on that cocky, arrogant, piece of shit Garcia.

Terri was having a bowl of cereal at the kitchen table when her helper of three years stepped through the door.

"Hi Esther, aren't we early this morning," Terri said sarcastically, smiling over her bowl. Esther normally showed for work at seven-thirty.

"Morning Miss Terri, sorry mi late but there was trouble in my neighbourhood this morning," Esther said as she went into the guest room to change into her housedress.

Terri nodded sympathetically. Esther lived in the inner city community of Grants Pen, which was a very volatile area. She had once been grazed by a bullet while on a sting operation there last year. Terri finished up her light breakfast and tried calling Anna again. Still her phone rang without an answer. She must have had a whale of a time last night to still be sleeping Terri mused, Anna was usually an early riser. Terri grabbed her keys and headed out the door. She had a few errands to run and she planned to stop by the office to get some work done.

Anthony headed out to the garage and decided to drive the black Cadillac Escalade. It seated eight people comfortably and while he didn't know how many people would be accompanying Hernandez, he figured that whoever couldn't hold in this truck could ride with Gavin the lawyer, who was to meet him at the harbour at five minutes to twelve. He checked the time as he exited the garage, Mayweather should be calling him any minute now. He would get a bite to eat now, then locate and terminate the security guard and then head out to the pier. Mayweather called him with the information ten minutes later. The guard lived off Eastwood Park road in the Half-Way-Tree area. Anthony called the number Mayweather gave him. A man answered on the third ring.

"Hello."

"Mr. Allen, this is Assistant Police Commissioner Mayweather, are you at home?" Anthony said in a serious, businesslike tone.

"Yes, sir," the man replied.

"I have some questions to ask you regarding the murder of Barry Laylor, stay at home until I get there; I'll be there in twenty minutes," Anthony said and hung up the phone. Craig Allen was surprised at getting a call from the Commissioner; he had hoped that if they had wanted to talk to him again it would have been the pretty police woman who was always on TV. He suddenly remembered that she had given him a card with a cell number on it and he decided to call and see if she would be accompanying the Commissioner.

He retrieved the card from his wallet and dialed her mobile number. She answered immediately. "Hello, Detective Corporal Miller here."

"Detective Miller, dis is Craig Allen, de security guard from Barry Laylor business place," Craig said excitedly.

"How may I help you Mr. Allen?" Terri asked pleasantly, hoping that he had some new information for her.

"Ah was jus' checkin' if you was coming here with the Commissioner, Ma'am," Craig intoned hopefully, he would love to see her again close up.

"With the Commissioner..? Come where Mr. Allen?" Terri asked, surprised and confused by what the man said.

"Him just call me say him on him way to see me to ask mi some questions bout Missa Laylor murda, so I was wondering if yuh was coming too," he replied.

Terri's brain was churning as she digested what he told her. This made absolutely no sense. Even if he was on the island why would the Commissioner be going to see Craig Allen?

"Oh yes, *that* meeting, remind me of your address again, I have it at the office but I'll be late if I have to go there before meeting the Commissioner at your house," Terri said after a moment's pause. It didn't make sense to alarm him until she knew what was going on.

He gave her the address happily. Terri was in the Liguanea area, about thirty minutes away. She aborted her original plan of stopping by her favourite boutique to pick up something new and sped down Hope Road. She dialed Mayweather's number. The man had said the Comissioner but the Commissioner was off the island so it had to be Mayweather, the Assistant Commissioner to whom he was referring. Mayweather's gravelly voice came over the line.

"Hello."

"Its Cpl. Miller sir," Terri said, "Did you call the security guard from the Laylor case today?"

Mayweather was silent for a few seconds as he wondered why she would ask that question. "No I haven't, what is this about Miller?" he demanded harshly.

"Well somebody pretending to be you did, and they are on their way to see him now. I'm heading there right now to see what the hell is going on, see if there are units close by and dispatch them to his house. He might be in danger." Terri replied as she navigated through the not-as-yet heavy Saturday morning traffic.

That stupid asshole, Mayweather fumed, why the fuck did he use my name. Aloud he said, "That is strange, I'll send a unit there immediately. Call me as soon as you hear anything further."

"Will do sir," Terri said and dialed the number that had come up on her caller ID when the guard had called her.

Anthony pulled up in front of gate number 17. The house was a bit rundown and in need of a serious paint job. He alighted from the vehicle quickly. There were a few cars passing on the road but no one was in the immediate vicinity. Anthony pushed the gate and entered the unkempt yard. The door opened and a short, rather ugly man stepped onto the veranda. Him look young fi be Commissioner, Craig Allen thought as he scrutinized the young, well-dressed man approaching him.

"Craig Allen?" the man said questioningly as he took a quick glance around.

"Yeah…" Craig responded nervously, feeling uneasy. The man did not even sound like a Jamaican.

"Let's go inside, I have a few things to clear up with you," the man said.

Craig Allen's cell phone rang as he backed up into the dusty living room. "Don't answer that," the man commanded as he shut the door behind him.

"Jus' a second, I think is the detective calling me back," Craig implored hastily and turned to pick up the phone off the worn sofa. Anthony stepped up to him quickly and shoved a long, thin blade in the back of his neck, the tip protruded from the other side. Blood leaked from his throat and neck rapidly. Anthony then kicked his twitching body forward and shot him in the head twice. The gunshots were a quiet thud. Craig Allen's body stopped moving. The cell phone was still ringing. Anthony clicked the answer button but said nothing.

"Mr. Allen? Craig? Are you there?" Terri asked hurriedly.

Anthony hung up and slipped the phone in his pocket. Detective Miller, Anthony thought, her voice ringing in his head as he exited the house. No one was paying him any attention. As he drove off, his cell phone rang. It was Mayweather.

"What the fuck are you thinking man?" Mayweather demanded furiously, "Why did you call the guard and use my name, you fucking idiot!"

Anthony's eyes glazed over with anger. You're a dead man Mayweather he thought. You just don't know it yet. Aloud he said, "Shut the fuck up Mayweather, and watch your mouth. Everything is cool."

"You shut the...."

Anthony hung up the phone and decided on a whim to stop at Flowers R Us. He purchased a bouquet of Orchids and paid for it to be delivered to Terri at police headquarters. He figured she would be there at some point during the day. Anthony then drove to The Taj; they had a nice breakfast buffet until eleven-thirty. It was only ten-fifteen. He could relax and have a meal before heading out to the harbour.

Mayweather was furious. That stupid, trigger-happy punk, he fumed as he paced his office. He needed to plan the best way to execute all of them. Hernandez was coming in today and would definitely want to meet with him. After he got an idea of what their immediate plans were, then he would proceed.

Terri pulled up at Craig Allen's house, surprised not to see any squad cars. She exited the car quickly and pulled her firearm. She was positive there was foul play. That was not Craig Allen breathing in the phone when she called. She held the gun low and stepped onto the veranda. She tried the door and found it unlocked. She pushed it open quickly and stepped in with her gun pointed straight ahead. She gasped when she saw a man's body face down on the sofa covered with blood with a knife embedded in the back of his neck. She checked the other rooms to make sure the house was empty and then she called headquarters to send a team down. She stood quietly, digesting the crime scene as she waited for the team to arrive. Why did the killer suddenly decide to kill him now? There was ample opportunity on the morning the murders were committed so why now? Terri called Mayweather to update him on the situation and to query what happened to the officers she had asked him to dispatch to the scene. If that had been done the poor man probably wouldn't be lying dead in a pool of blood.

Anthony gave the dead man's cell phone to a smiling street urchin who had attempted to wash his windows at the stop light. He pulled up at The Taj a few minutes later and put together a plate of fried plantains, liver and fried breadfruit from the scrumptious buffet. The place was relatively empty, just a handful of families and a few couples. He was the only person seated alone at a table. His cell phone rang while he was devouring his meal. It was Gavin, the lawyer.

"Just touching base with you Tony," he said. "Everything ok?"

"Yeah, it's all good. I'll see you at the harbour," Anthony replied as he drank some more orange juice. He ended the call and his mind drifted to Terri. She was probably at the crime scene now, pissed that she got there too late. He figured that she had been on her way there when she had called. Probably trying to warn the stupid guard that whoever was coming to see him was not the police. Hernandez would not be amused if he found out I liked this cop, Anthony mused as he took a bite of the breadfruit, whatever; he got off on danger. He wondered why he was so taken by her. It was more than her pretty face, he was used to that. Cuba had some of the most beautiful women in the world. Matter of fact, he was certain Hernandez was coming with a harem. Only thing Hernandez loved more than money was having beautiful women around him. After business was taken care of there would be a lot of fun tonight.

Pablo Hernandez sipped some bottled water as he relaxed between two lovely, half naked women in the back of his black stretch limo. They watched music videos on the two DVD screens as the limo crawled in the dense downtown Havana traffic. They were on their way to the marina where his luxurious yacht, *El Jefe*, was docked. The weather was great so he decided to sail to Jamaica rather than fly; besides the yacht had every amenity possible so it might be useful to have it docked there just in case, one never knows what might happen. Pablo was in an expansive mood. Two huge shipments of cocaine with a street value of over fifty million US dollars had made it safely through to Miami this week. Things were tight in recent times. With the new terror threat facing the United States, it was becoming increasingly difficult to get his product into the country. He had lost over sixty million in revenue since the September 11 attacks in the US. Counter-narcotics enforcement initiatives implemented by the US, UK, Latin American and Caribbean countries had also severely impacted the cocaine trade, driving the price sky high. However, there was still a tremendous amount of cocaine being shipped through Jamaica and Hernandez planned to be responsible for at least eighty percent of the trade through Jamaica. He had information on all the major players and which cop and government official they were backed by. He planned to use Wild Apache's soldiers to eliminate those players. The corrupt government officials and cops don't care who is pushing the product as long as they got their cut. Real estate was booming in Jamaica as well and he planned to discuss obtaining some land in Negril and Ocho Rios with Gavin, his trusted Jamaican lawyer. Maybe start a hotel chain or something geared towards Hispanic tourists. Hernandez sighed as one of the women started to feed him some fruit cocktail. Life was good.

Terri did not reach Mayweather on his cell and was told that he had left the office. When the team arrived, they secured the scene and processed the evidence under Terri's supervision. When they were through, she returned Anna's call. Anna had called while she was in the middle of instructing the team so she had told her she would have to call her back in a few.

"Hello," Anna said, her mouth sounding full when Terri returned her call.

"Hi greedy bug, what are you stuffing your face with?" Terri asked, wishing she could eat as much as Anna did and not worry about gaining weight.

"Pizza," she responded through a mouthful of pepperoni and cheese. "How was last night?" Terri asked as she leaned against her car. There was a small crowd loitering near the house. Word of the murder had spread fast and a bunch of curious onlookers had gathered to watch the proceedings.

"It was great. I went home with this investment banker from Trinidad. Girl, he ate me like I was roti," Anna said chuckling. "I came three times." Terri laughed. "You little slut, I had a nice session with Kunta last night." Kunta is her ribbed, jet black vibrator.

Anna laughed and asked her what happened to the cute Spanish guy. They chatted for a few more minutes then Terry told her she had some important things to do and would catch up with her later. She tried back Mayweather's number.

"Hello," he said.

"I've been trying to reach you, sir," Terri advised him, certain that he had seen the missed calls on his phone. Why hadn't he returned her calls?

"I got caught up with a situation," he replied evenly. "What's the status?"

"Craig Allen was murdered mere minutes before I got there. The killer even answered his cell phone when I called trying to warn him," Terri said.

"What did he say?" Mayweather asked.

"Nothing, he just listened then hung up," She replied, adding, "What happened to the officers I requested to be dispatched at the scene? No one was there when I arrived."

"Really? I did send a unit out. I'll follow up as to why they weren't there when you arrived," Mayweather responded.

He's lying. "I'll deal with them, just advise me which unit it was," Terri said.

"I'll handle it detective, you do your job and I'll do mine," Mayweather told her sternly.

"Ok sir." Terri was very disturbed. The Assistant Commissioner of Police is somehow mixed up in this case. Why would someone call the guard pretending to be Mayweather? Why did Mayweather not send the unit to the scene? She would have to tread carefully but she would get to the bottom of this.

Anthony arrived at the harbour in Port Royal a few minutes early. He went over to the bar and purchased a cold energy drink. He never drank alcohol before twelve. The bartender attempted to make small talk but Anthony ignored him. Gavin Wilkinson arrived a few moments later. Anthony watched him as he parked his Mercedes sedan and came over.

"Hey Tony," He said giving Anthony a friendly slap on the shoulder.

"You're late," Anthony responded, puffing on his cigar. Anthony looked at his cheap, ill-fitting suit in disgust. For a man with wealth Gavin sure dressed like a bum.

"Yeah, but so is Hernandez," Gavin said, and ordered a cold beer. The midday heat was sweltering. Gavin knew Garcia wasn't much of a talker so they sipped their beverages in silence as they waited for the yacht to land. There were two boats out on the horizon and Anthony figured one of them was El Jefe.

Hernandez had gotten Mayweather to see to it that the coast guard did not interfere with him once he entered Jamaican waters. Ten thousand US dollars and there's no record of them being in the country. Hernandez went below deck to change when the yacht was only a couple hundred yards from the harbour.

Anthony and Gavin walked down to the pier when the boat docked. They watched as the party exited the luxurious yacht. The two brothers, Juan and Carlos were the first to disembark. They did a little bit of everything for Hernandez. They were bodyguards, enforcers, errand boys, whatever Hernandez required. They were followed by four gorgeous women dressed in bikini tops and sarongs. Juan and Carlos greeted Anthony with handshakes and nodded at Gavin. The women smiled at Anthony and introduced themselves to him. This is a good batch the old man put together, Anthony mused as he looked at them appreciatively. Then Hernandez, dressed in a full white linen set, flanked by two tall, voluptuous women, completed the exodus.

"Tony," Hernandez said, greeting him with a hug.

"Padre, good to see you," Anthony replied.

He shook Gavin's hand and motioned for everyone to get the luggage together and load up the vehicles. While that was being done he chatted with the boat crew and gave them instructions. When every thing was set, he hopped his portly, five-nine frame into the passenger side of the Escalade and Anthony sped off with Gavin trailing in the Mercedes. Hernandez had told four of the women to ride with Gavin.

"So, we go up to the house, chill out for a bit and then we all go have dinner," Hernandez said to Anthony as he lit a cigar.

"Cool," Anthony replied, adding, "When do you want to meet with Wild Apache?"

"Tomorrow. That prick Mayweather wants to meet tonight. He was complaining about that incident today," Hernandez told him.

"Fuck him," Anthony snarled, "His days are numbered. We can buy another cop."

"Take it easy," Hernandez said soothingly. "He's number two in the chain of command. That won't be too easy to replace. So for now just try to get along." Anthony didn't respond. That cop was dead, no matter what Hernandez said.

Gavin was enjoying himself with the four beautiful exotic women riding with him. He had struck up a conversation with them and discovered that only one of them spoke English. So he regaled her with exaggerated stories of his exploits in the courtroom and the big clients he represented. The women looked around chattering excitedly. It was their first visit to Jamaica.

They pulled up at the Stony Hill mansion fifty minutes later. The men took the luggage upstairs and then Gavin left, promising to meet them for dinner later that evening at Roosters, Kingston's latest hot spot for dining. Hernandez and Anthony lounged by the poolside while Juan and Carlos played with some of the women in the large pool. Anthony noticed that the tall, quiet woman with the Cindy Crawford mole, stayed close to Hernandez at all times. Apparently she was his new favourite. She was now massaging his shoulders lightly, looking at Anthony with a stoic expression.

Anthony gave Hernandez an in-depth report on everything that he had accomplished since arriving three days ago. Hernandez chastised him lightly for not killing the security guard on the day he killed Laylor but he was pleased at how the meeting went with Wild Apache. Hernandez in turn filled him in on the success of the Miami shipments and other business matters. Anthony noticed how freely he talked business in front of the woman, Maria. That was not like him. He must be pussy-whipped Anthony thought. Anthony checked his watch and told Hernandez he was going to relax before dinner.

He gestured to the curvy blonde-haired woman in the tan bikini. She smiled and exited the pool, water dripping from her bronze-complexioned skin. Anthony took her hand and they went upstairs to his room.

Terri was surprised to see the flowers on the desk when she arrived at her office. She read the card. *I've been thinking about you. A lot. Hope you like the flowers. Tony.* Terri smiled. It would take a bit more for him to get into her pants but he was definitely on the right track. She would call him later. She was knee-deep in some paperwork when her phone rang. She smiled when she heard her mom's voice. She chatted to both her parents for a bit and promised to meet them at church in the morning. Her parents worshiped at the Catholic Church on Red Hills road. Terri accompanied them to church at least once a month; or tried to anyway. She reclined in her comfortably worn leather chair and let her mind wander a bit. Idly, she dialed the number of the security guard's cell phone. The phone had not been in the house when the crime scene was processed. The phone rang three times before someone answered.

"Hallo." A young man, early teens or younger.

"Hi, listen to me carefully and don't hang up," Terri said softly in her most trusting voice. "This phone was stolen. Now I don't want it back, just tell me how you got it." She hoped the kid wouldn't panic and hang up.

"Ah nuh mi tief yuh phone miss," the boy retorted.

"I know it wasn't you," Terri replied quickly, "just tell me how you got the phone."

"Is a man gimme today," he said.

"Ok, can you describe this man?" Terri asked hopefully.

"Him brown and have money," the boy replied.

"Why do you say he has money?" Terri asked.

"Cause him drive pretty car," the boy said in a tone that suggested he thought it was a stupid question.

"What kind of car was it?"

"Black. Ah black escalade like weh DJ Snapper drive," the boy said, referring to a popular Jamaican recording artiste.

"Thank you very much. One more thing, about what time was this?"

"Inna de morning, him stop at de stop light an' mi try fi wash him window but him stop mi and throw de phone give mi."

"Ok, thank you young man," Terri said and ended the call.

Terri mentally assessed the case. It was obvious that the person who killed Laylor was the same person who killed the security guard. The spent shells at both scenes came from the same gun. He owned or had access to expensive vehicles; first a Range Rover, now an Escalade. He was a professional killer; his weapon had a silencer, no one had heard any shots fired in either of the murders. He liked to take chances; he answered the man's cell phone and then casually gave it away. He was bold; both killings in broad daylight with a fair degree of risk involved. Where did Mayweather fit into all this? Hopefully when she received Laylor's phone records on Monday it would help to fit together a few pieces in the puzzle.

Wild Apache and two of his most trusted henchmen were seated in his den eating a dinner of curry goat and boiled dumplings, prepared by one of Wild Apache's common law wives. He lived with three women.

"De Spanish druggist come in today," he advised them, chomping noisily on his food. "Mi ago meet wid him tomorrow and him supposed to give we a deposit fi get the ball rolling. Ten thousand US." It was actually fifteen thousand but what's the point of being in charge if yuh nuh keep a ting fi yuself? Wild Apache mused.

"Dat good," the one everyone called Scarface said. He had an ugly scar on his left jaw, courtesy of a skirmish with a rival gang member in prison several years ago.

"So what a de first move?" Reds queried. He was a mulatto who loved nothing more than to fire his gun. Wild Apache respected him because he was always ready for action.

"Some coke deh over Jungle. Whole heap. Bout sixteen kilo. Dem a get it ready fi send it ah England. We ago tek dat tomorrow night," Wild Apache informed them, adding, "an' we ago kill Benjie Dread." Benjie Dread was the leader of the Rasta Rascals, the gang that ruled the ghetto of Jungle with an iron fist.

Reds belched loudly after taking a long drink of the sour sop juice that Wild Apache's woman had made. "Sound good, real good," he said grinning. He hadn't shot anyone since last week.

CHAPTER 5

A t seven o' clock that night, Hernandez and his party piled into the Escalade and the BMW, and set off for Roosters where they were to have dinner. Gavin had made the reservations and was to meet them there. Hernandez rode in the back of the BMW with Maria, with the top down, while Anthony drove. The woman he had sex with earlier that afternoon rode shot gun. Carlos followed in the Escalade along with his brother and the other five women. Anthony drove at a moderate pace, allowing Carlos to keep up with him easily as Carlos was not familiar with the Jamaican roads.

The party of ten was an impressive looking bunch when they strolled into the trendy restaurant. The women were gorgeous and sexily clad, while the men looked resplendent in their blazers and slacks. People stared at the group openly. The maitre d' led them to their two reserved tables where Gavin was waiting. Hernandez, Gavin, Anthony and Maria sat at one table, while the brothers and the other five women sat at the larger table. Anthony was getting more and more annoyed at the way Hernandez always had to have Maria at his side, even when sensitive matters were being discussed. She was really gorgeous though, Anthony thought as he admired her discreetly. Her make-up was flawless. Her large almond-shaped eyes were sultry and looked as if they held secrets to which not even the Kama Sutra was privy. Her full breasts defied gravity and the thin diamond necklace looked perfect around her elegant neck. It was impossible to guess her age. Hernandez ordered steak and potatoes, while Maria ordered a chicken salad. Anthony wanted fricassee chicken with rice and peas, while Gavin decided on lamb in lemon sauce. Hernandez also ordered a bottle of their finest champagne along with two bottles of red wine.

Business was the main topic of discussion at Anthony's table while at the other table the mood was more festive. Carlos and Juan entertained the five women with stories and songs as they all laughed and conversed in Spanish. Pablo took out his cell phone and dialed Mayweather's number.

Mayweather stood in his bedroom, clad in his briefs as he looked in the closet for something to put on. Where the fuck is my blue shirt he thought. That fucking bitch can't do anything right. "Elaine!" he shouted. "Where is my blue polo shirt?"

"It's in the wash Claude," Elaine responded from her perch on the sofa in the living room where she was reading a romance novel.

"How the rass that help me? I want it to put on now!" Mayweather said angrily.

Wear something else, you miserable prick Elaine thought. Aloud she said, "Remember the helper was ill last week Claude."

"Woman don't upset me. Yuh..." his cell phone rang, interrupting his tirade.

"Hello," Mayweather said in a gruff tone.

"Damn man, everytime I talk to you, you sound like a miserable old fart. You need to lighten up Mayweather," Hernandez said chuckling. "Swing by the mansion later. Anytime after nine. We'll talk business and I have a bevy of beauties available. You definitely sound like you could use some pussy." Hernandez laughed boisterously as he ended the call. Mayweather trembled with rage at the disrespectful way that Hernandez had spoken to him. It hadn't always been this way. When Gavin Wilkinson had introduced him to the Cuban gangster a year ago, he had found Hernandez to be an affable, likeable man with lots of US currency at his disposal. After a few meetings, he decided to accept Hernandez's offer to be on his payroll. All he had to do was provide the kind of information and protection that his post as Assistant Commissioner of Police could provide. The money was great and he had his future to think about. He was fifty-five and planning to retire in a couple of years. But things had turned for the worse in recent times. Hernandez and that cock-sucker Garcia started to treat him like he was their yard boy. They will definitely get what's coming to them, Mayweather vowed as he went out into the living room to vent his anger on his wife.

Elaine was just getting to the juicy sex scene in the romance novel she was reading when her husband stormed into the living room and swatted the book out of her hands. She looked up in fear as he stood over her menacingly. She glanced down at his crotch. The front of his white cotton briefs resembled a tent. The bastard got off on slapping her around.

"Claude..." Elaine began, screaming as he grabbed a fistful of her hair and slapped her viciously across her cheek. He then pushed her to her knees and freed his erection. She sobbed as she fellated her husband who began thrusting excitedly in her mouth. An hour later after he had left the house, Elaine was still on the floor by the sofa, her face messy with tears and semen. She now knew what she had to do.

Terri got home at eight that night. She was beat. A nice long bath followed by a good meal and a slow, lengthy session of mind-blowing sex would be nice. The first two were readily available and to be honest, so was the third. All she had to do was call Anthony. She reminisced on last night when they kissed as she took off her clothes. He was a very good kisser. A man who kisses well is usually a good lover. Terri sighed and went into the bathroom to take a bubble bath. She carried the cordless phone with her to call Anthony.

Anthony was sipping on a glass of champagne and half-listening to Hernandez's stale jokes that he had heard a million times when his cell phone rang. He looked on the caller ID. It was Terri.

"Hi sexy," Anthony said.

"Thank you for the flowers Tony, they were lovely," Terri told him.

"Is that water I hear splashing?" Anthony asked; ignoring the questioning glance Hernandez was throwing his way.

Damn, he has ears like an eagle. I barely moved my legs just now. "Yes, I'm taking a bath. A bubble bath."

"Mmmm, wish I was there to wash your back," Anthony said, in a tone so wistful that Terri felt her nipples harden.

She cleared her throat. "Only my back?" she asked softly.

"Terri...stop before I rip a hole in my slacks," Anthony replied half-jokingly. The image of her in naked in the tub had given him an instant erection. "When can I see you?"

Terri thought a moment before responding. "Well, I'm going to church tomorrow morning, and then I plan to spend a few hours at the beach. You're welcome to accompany me, to both."

"I'll pass on the church but it's a date for the beach. Call me," Anthony told her, as he noticed Maria watching him.

"Will do. Bye Tony."

"You look like a man *en amor* Tony," Hernandez teased when Anthony came off the phone. "Who is she?"

"This chick I met the other day," Anthony said nonchalantly.

"This puta must be something eh," Hernandez said laughing, "turning a killer into a pussycat."

The others around the table laughed as Anthony smiled and sipped his champagne. Look who's talking he thought. Since you arrived you've been wearing Maria like a second skin, Anthony mused. Hernandez signaled for the cheque when the champagne was finished. He left a generous fifty percent tip and they left the restaurant and sauntered out into the cool night air. Gavin decided to accompany them to the mansion. He hung possessively to the arm of the black-haired beauty who had ridden in the front of his car from the mariner and they hopped in his Mercedes. The three vehicles pulled off and made their way to Stony Hill. When they arrived at the mansion, the woman motioned for Gavin to follow her to the pool. She slid out of her dress and told Gavin to join her. He hesitated at first then stripped off his clothes, leaving on his boxers. She reached for him as he entered the pool. She immediately understood why he didn't want to expose himself. He had a small *carajo*. It didn't matter. They were here to cater to any-one associated with Hernandez. Hernandez watched them from the balcony outside his master bedroom. He heard his toilet flush and felt Maria's arms around him moments later. He moaned when she slid her tongue in his ear and turned away from the thrashing couple in the pool. She led him to the king size bed and performed the skills that had promoted her from being just another puta for hire.

Assistant Commissioner of Police Claude Mayweather arrived at the mansion at ten o' clock. Everyone was in the living room watching the title bout between the rising Hispanic star Hector Ruiz and the American southpaw Floyd Andrews. It was the final round of a scheduled twelve and the scorecards were even to this point.

The front door was open so Mayweather just stepped right in. He bade everyone a curt goodnight but instantly mellowed out when he saw how beautiful the women were. Hernandez wasn't lying he thought as one of the women got up and indicated for him to sit so she could sit in his lap. The fight was exciting, both boxers were giving it their all but Mayweather could only think of the supple, scantily clad beauty in his lap. She felt his erection and discreetly adjusted herself so that she sat directly on it. Mayweather almost creamed in his pants.

Two minutes later, the fight was over and the group was cheering as the Spanish guy had won. He was from Puerto Rico but it didn't matter. They were all Latino. Hernandez then stood up and told Mayweather to walk with him out to the poolside. Anthony also followed. The three men reclined at the poolside and Maria emerged a few minutes later with a six pack of ice cold coronas. She then went behind Hernandez and lightly massaged his shoulders. Mayweather struggled to keep his eyes off her.

"So," Hernandez began, "I'll be here for awhile and things are already in motion. The body count across Kingston will be rising over the next couple of weeks. We expect the usual reports from you on any police investigation related to my operations. And of course, your interference in such investigations where necessary."

"No problem," Mayweather replied, adding, "The assistance the government requested from Britain will be here next month." He took a swig of the beer and continued, "You guys will have to tread carefully and cover your tracks. Things won't be the same when I have Scotland Yard here snooping around. Between them and that bitch Terri Miller, we can't afford to slip up."

"Who the fuck is Terri Miller?" Hernandez asked.

"She's a nosy cop who has a knack for solving cases. The *top* detective in Jamaica," Mayweather said derisively.

"Well, if she's a problem, I'll just have her terminated," Hernandez responded dismissively.

"Slow your roll Hernandez," Mayweather said seriously, "If she was to be murdered they would leave no stone unturned in finding her killers. She's a fucking hero to the Jamaican people."

"I'll kill anyone who poses a threat to my business," Hernandez said matter-of-factly, "You remember that Mayweather."

Anthony gave Mayweather a smirk. He was glad to see that Hernandez still had his *cojones*. Thought maybe that bitch Maria was making him lose his focus. Mayweather looked at both of them and sipped his beer. He would meet with his special unit tomorrow to plan their execution. These fuckers were out of control. After business was concluded, Mayweather took up Hernandez on his offer of entertainment and anxiously followed the nubile girl who had sat in his lap earlier to her room.

When they were both naked she whispered something in Spanish he didn't understand but by the look on her face he could tell she was impressed by his size. Yeah, the old boy still got it Mayweather thought smugly as he rolled on a rubber and entered her from behind, eschewing any foreplay.

"Ohh papi!" she moaned as Mayweather gripped her tightly around her waist and pounded her petite body. Terri Miller has no idea what the hell she's missing Mayweather thought as he changed positions and allowed her to straddle him. "Oohhh, estoy por acabar!" she squealed as she rode him feverishly. He didn't understand a word she was saying but he could feel that she just had an orgasm. She slumped on his hairy chest moaning softly. Mayweather flipped her over and resumed his assault. She got back into it and met his thrusts eagerly. Fifteen minutes later, Mayweather bid his hosts goodnight and headed home; completely spent.

He thought about his wife as he drove his four year old Land Rover home. Twelve long years they've been married. He had liked the shy, naïve country girl who had started out as a secretary at police headquarters and quickly swept her off her feet. They got married seven months after meeting. Things had started out well enough and aside from the occasional squabble that all married couples go through, things were pretty much ok. But over the past six years she had let herself go and had gotten fat and sloppy. Though she was nine years his junior, at fifty-five his sex drive was roaring while she was content to have sex a couple times for the month. What had started out as an occasional slap had now become routine. Lately he couldn't even get hard unless he slapped her around. Mayweather sighed as he turned onto his street. Oh well, she was his cross to bear. For better or for worse he had uttered at the altar.

Anthony felt bored. Hernandez was out cold from either the liquor or Maria's loving or maybe both. Gavin was around somewhere with one of the girls; the brothers were locked down with two of the other girls and he had no appetite for the one he slept with last night. The cute petite one that had fucked Mayweather was now watching TV but he was not interested in touching anything that Mayweather had been inside of. Anthony checked the time. It was 11:30. He wondered what Terri was doing. Anthony lit a cigar and walked past the pool to the clump of trees that were at the back of the property. He was shirtless and the light breeze felt cool on his bare skin. He heard quiet footsteps behind him and spun around with his gun drawn. It was Maria. He lowered his gun and put it back in the holster. She had on a sweater that stopped a little above her knees, and sandals. Her hair was tousled and seemed wet. She must have just come out the shower.

"Be careful walking up on me like that," Anthony said, looking at the swell of her ample bosom underneath her sweater in the bright moon light.

"I like living dangerously," came the soft reply.

"What do you want Maria?" Anthony asked.

"Same thing you want," she answered.

"And what might that be?"

"Everything."

Anthony frowned. "Don't play games with me woman," he said sternly.

"I have something to tell you. Something I think you should know."

Anthony said nothing.

"Sometimes when Hernandez and I are in bed, after sex, especially when he had been drinking, he talks a lot. Just now he told me something about you. About your mother."

Anthony tensed but remained silent.

Maria continued, "He told me that your mother had been a prostitute, but she had been a beautiful, high class whore. She only did business with men who had lots of *enchilada*. He had taken a liking to her back when he had just started making major money and basically moved her in with him. One day he received information that when he was away on business she had fucked one of his rivals. When he confronted her she told him it was only business, not personal. Enraged, he had beaten her badly, disfiguring her face and allowed his bodyguards to do whatever they wanted to her sexually. They even sodomized her. Then Hernandez injected her with heroin and they dropped her off at a roadside in Havana. Someone saw her bloody and unconscious on the road and took her to the hospital. She recovered from the ordeal, but her face was ruined and she had no money, just the clothes on her back. So she started selling her body again, this time operating from the street corner and down by the harbours, to anyone who would fuck her. That's how she met your father, a Jamaican fisherman. Apparently he fucked her without protection and she got pregnant. The rest you already know. She never fully kicked her drug habit and died from an overdose when you were eleven."

Maria paused, and looked away in the distance. "That's one of the reasons why he took you in. When he saw your face that day at his villa, he realized that you were Penelope's child. You look just like her."

Anthony took a deep breath and forced himself to remain calm; otherwise he would march up to Hernandez's room, wake him and shoot him in places that would cause him to die a slow and painful death. The man he had been loyal to all these years and loved like a father had been responsible for his mother's suffering and eventual death. The images of what Maria had described to him played in his head like a horror flick. Hernandez would pay, Anthony vowed silently, and pay dearly. To Maria, who had been standing there quietly, watching him with pensive eyes, he said softly, "Thank you for telling me."

"It was the right thing to do," she replied.

Anthony stood there deeply wrapped in his own thoughts for over an hour after Maria had quietly withdrawn and went back to the house. It was now 12.45 but he was too tense to go to sleep. He decided to get dressed and go on the road. Fifteen minutes later, dressed in full black, Anthony hopped in the black Escalade and headed down to New Kingston. He lit a cigar as he drove down Waterloo road; he really needed to release some tension. Waterloo road was a popular hangout for prostitutes at night. Anthony drove slowly as he looked at the wares on display. They were going all out to get his attention, the shiny black escalade indicating that the occupant had money. They made lewd cat calls and some of them freed their ample breasts as he cruised by, giving him a preview of what they had to offer. One woman caught his eye. She was jet black and extremely voluptuous. She stood off a bit from the rest of the women. She was tall, about five-eleven, had thighs that looked like they would squeeze the life out of somebody and huge breasts that were propped up alluringly by the push up bra under her close fitting white dress. Her hair was in braids and pulled back in a chignon. Anthony pulled up at the curb. Normally he would never solicit a street whore but the woman appealed to him. She strutted over to the SUV. Anthony put the window down and took a close look at her face. She was attractive. Her jet black skin was like onyx and her lips were full and inviting. She reminded him of that actress Angela Bassett; a cuter, darker version.

"Goodnight," she said in a husky tone.

"What's good about it?" Anthony asked.

"Well, if we go somewhere you'll find out," she responded as she peered into the large vehicle to check if he was alone.

"Motel…?" Anthony asked as he blew circles from his cigar.

"Sure, or we can go to my apartment. It's not far from here," she replied.

Anthony looked in his rear view mirror. A car had pulled up behind him and a light-skinned prostitute in a long blonde weave jogged over to the car and got in. They drove off immediately. "Ok, we'll go to your apartment," Anthony said, adding, "providing it's clean." If she was offended she didn't show it.

"It is," she replied and climbed into the vehicle. Anthony got a whiff of her perfume; it smelled expensive. He looked at her appraisingly before driving off. She was very thick but toned. Her stomach was flat and she had a tiny waist which further accentuated her lush, wide hips. She definitely wasn't your typical street prostitute he surmised as he drove off, he had chosen well.

They arrived at her apartment eight minutes later. Anthony was pleasantly surprised. It was a nice enough apartment in a housing complex off Hope road. It was small but clean and tastefully furnished. Anthony declined her offer for a drink and sat on the couch. She poured herself a glass of white wine and sat opposite him.

"I normally work out of my apartment but none of my regulars were coming tonight so I decided to hit the streets. A night without making money is a night wasted," she said and sipped her wine. Anthony didn't respond.

"So, what is it you require...anything special?" she asked, deciding to get down to business as the man didn't seem to be interested in small talk.

"Tell you what, I'll give you one hundred and fifty US dollars and you do whatever I want," Anthony replied.

"If that includes anal make it two hundred and we've got a deal," she responded, mentally calculating that two hundred would give her close to thirteen thousand Jamaican dollars. She wouldn't need to go back on the street for the rest of the night.

Anthony looked at her for a moment before responding; he didn't like to be hustled. She fidgeted a bit under his steely gaze. "Ok," he eventually said, and removed two crisp US hundred dollar bills from his wallet and held it out to her. She gently took it from his hands and excused herself. She reemerged ten minutes later dressed in a sexy black crotch-less negligee set. A pair of black stilettos completed the ensemble. Anthony stood and faced her. Her six inch heels made her tower a few inches above his six-foot-two-inch frame. She was an Amazon. I'll break you down to size, Anthony thought as he shrugged off his blazer. She was startled when she saw his gun in a holster under his right armpit but did not comment on the weapon.

"Come this way," she said, and turned to go into the bedroom. Anthony watched her voluptuous ass sway from side to side. It was almost hypnotic. The bedroom was dominated by a large bed with took up almost all the space in the room. The sheets were white and appeared freshly laundered. The light was low but bright enough for them to see everything. She slowly undressed Anthony and eased him onto the bed. She trailed soft, feathery kisses from his ankle to his inner thighs. By the time she took him in her mouth, the usually in control Anthony was squirming on the bed in pleasure. He thought he heard a sound in the living room but ignored it as being his imagination. She rolled a condom onto his turgid erection and slowly impaled herself on his shaft. Anthony groaned with pleasure but he felt slightly uneasy. He felt like someone else was in the apartment. He reached down by the bedside and gripped his handgun as she increased her tempo, her huge breasts bouncing mightily. Two men suddenly barged in the room. The prostitute screamed and jumped off Anthony as he deftly rolled off the bed and squeezed off six quick shots at the onrushing figures.

"Bumboclaat!" was the tortured cry from one of them as his body lurched back and he fell to the ground. The other one was quiet. Anthony got up slowly off the floor holding his gun steadily in front of him. He turned up the switch on the bedside lamp bathing the room in bright light. The prostitute was cowering on the floor around the other side of the bed peering up at Anthony while one of the men was writhing on the floor, blood leaking from his stomach and shoulder; a large knife was on the floor next to him. Anthony could only see the leg of the other one protruding from the other side of the bed. He walked over to the man closest to him and shot him in the face. He pulled the other man's leg and drew him out from under the bed. He was already dead; shot in the stomach.

"Get up and get over here," Anthony commanded, as he pulled the condom off his now flaccid dick. The prostitute fearfully stood up and approached him gingerly.

"I'm sorry…" she began tearfully as Anthony butted her in the forehead with his gun, cutting her off in mid sentence. He grabbed her by her extensions and told her to open her mouth. She quickly did as she was told and Anthony shoved the long, slender handgun in her mouth. She gagged on the silencer.

"So you want to set people up," he growled in her ear, "You trifling puta."

Her eyes were wide with terror as she shook her head from side to side, unable to speak with the gun in her mouth. Incredulously, her last thought was that he had eyes like a cat. Anthony squeezed the trigger and splattered her brains all over the white sheets. He then released her lifeless body to the floor. Anthony checked the time; it was two in the morning. He got dressed and retrieved the money he had paid the prostitute from a top dresser drawer. Anthony then hopped in the Escalade and headed home. He arrived at the mansion thirty minutes later. The house was in total darkness. He headed straight for the bathroom and jumped in the shower. When he went into his bedroom, the girl he had slept with the previous evening was waiting for him under the covers. He didn't mind, the prostitute's greed had led to coitus interruptus.

Later that morning, at six a.m., the prostitute's sister, Judy, who had moved to Kingston four weeks ago, and was staying with her sister until she got her own place, entered the apartment half drunk and went to the bedroom to get undressed. She sobered instantly when she reached the doorway. Judy screamed at the top of her lungs when she was greeted by the gruesome sight of the contents of her sister's head splattered all over the bed and the bloody bodies of two men. The neighbours rushed over to find her rooted at the doorway still screaming. They pulled her from the doorway and someone dialed 119.

Terri was getting ready to meet her parents at mass when she received the call on her cell phone from one of the inspectors under her direct supervision. She took off the dress she was about to wear to church and slipped into jeans, boots and a white shirt, and jumped in her car. Her parents were en route to church when she called them to let them know she wouldn't be able to make it.

When Terri arrived at the scene thirty-five minutes later, there was a large crowd outside the apartment, kept at bay by the police and the yellow tape placed at the entrance of the apartment. Terri entered the apartment and looked around as she got briefed by the detective who was first on the scene. She had seen her fair share of crime scenes but seeing the bloody half-naked woman with her brains all over the bed had to rank as one of the most gruesome sights she had ever seen. Terri analyzed the crime scene and tried to figure out what took place. The spent shells appeared to be from the same make weapon as the previous two murders but she would have to wait on the lab report to be absolutely sure. The detective had also informed her that one of the neighbours had seen a black SUV leaving the premises in the wee hours of the morning. The person didn't know what make vehicle it was but Terri was certain it was a black Escalade. Six murders in three days; this man had to be caught and caught quickly. Terri made a note to visit Waterloo Road later that night where the dead prostitute was said to ply her wares occasionally. Hopefully one of the women would have some helpful information. An hour and a half later, the bodies were removed and Terri gave a brief statement to the press who had arrived on the scene.

The living and dining room was a bed of activity when Anthony went downstairs at nine-thirty that morning. Hernandez was playing cards with Juan and Carlos and three of the girls were eating and watching fashion TV.

"Tony, had a long night eh," Hernandez commented when he looked up and saw him.

"Yeah, something like that," Anthony replied and went into the kitchen to see what the girls had prepared. He put together a plate of scrambled eggs and toast and poured a glass of orange juice. He went back into the living room and sat on the sofa. He ate quietly, gathering his thoughts.

"Tony, we are going to see Wild Apache later this evening," Hernandez told him as he shuffled the deck. "About four o'clock."

Anthony shoveled some eggs in his mouth and nodded. One of the girls got up and went upstairs, returning with a small bag of cocaine. She emptied the bag onto the glass top of the mahogany coffee table and made a neat line with the cocaine. She then took a hundred dollar bill from her shorts pocket, rolled it and snorted from the line. She then leaned back into the sofa, her eyes glazed like donuts. The other two finished what was left. Anthony finished eating and decided to take a swim. Maria was lying topless by the pool and the other two girls were swimming.

"Hey," Anthony said, stopping by Maria. Her breasts looked magnificent in the bright Sunday morning sunshine.

"Hi Tony," she said softly. "How are you feeling?" He looked at her for a moment. She looked genuinely concerned.

"I'm ok," Anthony replied. He then turned from her and dove in the deep end of the vast pool.

Anthony was floating and watching the two girls frolic in the pool when Hernandez came out there with Juan and Carlos in tow. He frowned when he saw Maria sunning topless. He went over there and said something to her and she sat up and put on her bikini top. He's truly pussy-whipped Anthony mused, thinking he just might fuck Maria and rub it in his face before he killed him. He sighed and hoped Terri called him early. He really wanted to see her before he had to head out to Rockfort with Hernandez to see Wild Apache.

Mayweather met with his special unit on his back porch over coffee and cigarettes at ten that morning. The unit consisted of four rogue cops; two veterans and two young cops with four years of service under their belt. They were involved in drug smuggling, extortion and murder. They answered only to him. He gave them a free rein to do as they wished; all they had to do was carry out whatever orders he gave them from to time. Now he needed them to execute Hernandez and his boys. They made tentative plans to go up to the mansion Tuesday night. Mayweather would confirm the exact time by Tuesday evening. Sergeant Peters was happy with this assignment. He had eight children and school would be re-opening in a couple weeks. The fee of two thousand US dollars plus his cut of whatever drugs and guns they retrieved from the mansion would definitely come in handy.

Terri got home from headquarters at 11 a.m. After leaving the crime scene, she had gone to her office to do up a report and to analyze the evidence. She left a few details out of the report, deciding it best to keep a few things close to her vest. Asst. Commissioner Mayweather could not be trusted. Terri made herself a bacon and cheese sandwich and put on her Luther Vandross CD. Still can't believe he's dead, she thought as she hummed the words to one of his many hit songs. Terri washed the sandwich down with some Gatorade and picked up the phone to call Anthony.

Anthony was cleaning his Beratta when his cell phone rang. He checked the caller ID and recognized Terri's number. "Hey sexy," Anthony drawled.

Terri felt a warm glow when she heard the smile in his voice. "Hi Tony," she purred.

"How was church?" Anthony asked, "Did you pray for me?"

"Unfortunately I didn't make it," she told him. "Had to work."

"Are we still on for the beach?"

"Yeah, which one would you like to go to?" Terri asked as she played with her hair.

"Any one," Anthony responded. "I just want to see you...spend some time with you."

She liked his earnest tone. "Ok, we'll decide when we're driving out. It can't be an out of town beach though; I've got some work to do in a couple hours."

"That's fine, so do I." Terri gave him her address and told him to pick her up in an hour. Terri lived in a gated townhouse complex in Stony Hill, not far from the mansion; Anthony could be there in five minutes. He got up and went to the bathroom, thinking it wouldn't be a good idea to let Terri know where he was staying. He could never let her come here. Forty minutes later, Anthony was dressed in a short-sleeved white shirt, white linen trousers and white Gucci loafers. A pair of Gucci sunglasses completed his outfit. His pistol was in its holster but he decided to keep it in the car because of the kind of shirt he was wearing.

"Tony, where ya headed all dressed up?" Hernandez enquired from his perch on the sofa when Anthony came into view. He was being fed grapes by Maria who was looking at Anthony with eyes that said you look good enough to eat.

"I'm gonna see someone for a bit," Anthony replied without breaking his stride.

"Remember we leave to see Wild Apache at four," Hernandez said to his retreating back.

Anthony briefly pondered which vehicle to drive; then hopped into the BMW. The sky was getting overcast so he kept the top up. When he arrived at the apartment complex the guard at the gate queried his intentions and buzzed him in. The complex housed ten three bedroom units and was clean and immaculately kept. Anthony pulled up behind Terri's sports car in the driveway at number three. He placed his firearm into the hidden compartment on the dashboard

50

and exited the vehicle. The rain started to drizzle lightly as he stepped up and rang her doorbell.

"Hi Tony," Terri said softly, adding, "You look great."

"Thanks, you don't look too bad yourself," he replied grinning. Terri punched him playfully on his arm and gestured for him to come in. Anthony took off his shades and pulled her close to him.

"No hug? What kind of way is that to greet your guest…" Anthony whispered as he held her in his arms. Her prominent nipples poked his chest through her bikini top. Terri sighed as he kissed her gently on her neck. God, that feels good, Terri thought inwardly. There was a loud clap of thunder and the rain came pouring down. Terri gently extricated herself from his embrace. "Guess our beach plans are ruined," she muttered, suddenly feeling nervous. What now?

Anthony nodded, noting her nervousness. "Look Terri, there's no doubt I'm feeling you like crazy, but there's no pressure. I'm content to just sit here and talk…and look at you." He traced her jaw line lovingly. He's so handsome…and sweet, Terri thought as she looked into his unusual grey eyes. Terri cleared her throat. "Ok, let's have a drink and relax on the patio outside my bedroom." Terri poured them some rum punch and they went upstairs. They passed through her large, antique-decorated bedroom and sat beside each other on the comfortable lounge chair. The awning kept the rain from wetting them. They talked about any and everything. Terri felt closer to him with each passing minute. She learned that Anthony was an orphan. That he grew up poor until his rich uncle took him in; Anthony helped his uncle run a successful business empire that spanned a pharmaceutical company, a funeral home and real estate holdings. Anthony told her of life in communist Cuba and that his mother had died of a drug overdose. In turn, Anthony learned of Terri's privileged background, her decision to become a cop and her experiences at the prestigious but racist University where she had studied abroad.

Terri glanced at her watch and was astonished that they had been talking non-stop for over two hours. He's so easy to talk to she thought, as she snuggled up to him on the chair. The rain had eased up a bit but the afternoon breeze was a bit chilly. Anthony hugged her to him and she could feel his erection poking her in the side. Her heartbeat accelerated. She wanted him but it was still too soon. It'd been only three days since they met. Sometimes she wished she wasn't so anal. She decided that if he pushed the issue she wouldn't back down. It's been too long since she got laid. She was tired of Kunta. It needed batteries anyway.

Anthony bent his head and gently licked her earlobe. Terri shivered. She clutched his shirt as he slowly nuzzled her neck. That was one of her spots. She moaned. He continued, nipping her gently with his teeth. Her pussy throbbed. Anthony emitted a low growl and carried her in his arms to the queen size bed. Terri didn't resist. Anthony pulled her sarong. Her red bikini had a large wet spot at the crotch. He slowly eased it down her curvy hips. Anthony groaned when he saw her pussy. It was clean shaven and plump as a peach. It glistened with her juices. Anthony discarded her bikini top and her full breasts sprang free. Her nipples stood proudly at attention.

Terri trembled with anticipation and a little bit of anxiety as she watched Anthony undress slowly. He was ripped and toned to perfection. You could use his abs in a bowflex commercial, she mused in lustful admiration. She liked the large tattoo on his chest; looked like a cobra entangled in a fight with a panther. He took off his linen trousers and stepped out of his silk boxers. His erection looked hard as steel. Terri opened her arms and he fell into them, taking one of her nipples in his mouth. She groaned and caressed his back. They kissed and groped each other feverishly. Anthony trailed wet kisses down her stomach and Terri moaned loudly when she felt his tongue inside her wetness.

"Sweet Jesus...," Terri blurted when he began to suck on her clit. "Oh god...Tony...don't...stop...please...I'm...coming." Terri clamped her thighs tightly, holding Anthony's head firmly in place as intense spasms rocked her body. When she finally released his head, he rose and retrieved a rubber from his pants. He got behind her and positioned them so they were lying on their sides. Then he entered her. She grabbed a pillow and bit into it as Anthony slowly thrust in and out. He gave her long deep strokes.

"Your pussy feels sooo good," Anthony whispered in her ear. "It tastes even better." Terri wasn't used to men talking dirty to her in bed. She liked it. A lot. She joined in.

"Fuck me Tony," She moaned. "Fill me up with that dick."

Anthony flipped her on her back and entered her in the missionary position and pushed her legs back until her ankles touched her ears. Terri groaned loudly. She felt delightfully filled. He was in so deep.

"Who's fucking you?" Anthony demanded as he increased his tempo.

"Tony...."

"Who?!"

"Tony!"

"Who this pussy belongs to?!"

"Tony! Ohhh!" Terri came so hard she felt faint. It was the first time she had ever climaxed from penetration.

Anthony plunged into her rapidly and grunted as he climaxed. Breathing heavily, he got up and rolled off the condom. He went into the bathroom. She watched him as he urinated. He also had a tattoo across his back; R.I.P. PENELOPE. His mother. She sighed contentedly as he came back to bed. He sat and stroked her face.

"That was phenomenal Tony," Terri breathed.

"You're definitely something Ms. Miller," Anthony said smiling. Terri got up and got on her knees before him. He watched as his flaccid penis disappeared in her mouth. She removed it and pulled the foreskin back several times, licking the tip gently. It grew rapidly in her hand. Anthony groaned and grabbed a fistful of her hair. She didn't stop until he came. Thirty minutes later, Anthony checked the time. He needed to get back to the mansion.

"Baby, I've got to go. My uncle and I have to meet with some people in a few," he told her as they lay in each others arms. The rain had stopped and a late afternoon sun was peeping out.

"Ok Tony," she replied softly. "I have some work to do as well, but that's later this evening."

"I'll call you later." He kissed her and got up to get dressed. Terri slipped on a robe and walked him to the door. He slipped a finger inside her and tasted it. She blushed. Anthony grinned and hopped into his car. Terri went back to bed. The scent of their passionate love making permeated the room. The dick was too good to keep to herself. She dialed Anna's number.

CHAPTER 6

When Anthony returned to the mansion, the women were already dressed and lounging downstairs. Except for Maria. She was most likely still upstairs with Hernandez. Juan and Carlos were in the kitchen arguing about who was currently the best basketball player in the world. Anthony nodded a greeting to the women and went upstairs to take a shower. He emerged downstairs at exactly four o' clock. Everyone was just about ready to go. They piled into the Range Rover and the Escalade and pulled out. The Range Rover had not been driven since Mayweather had informed Anthony that the vehicle was hot; but with the security guard now dead, if worse came to worse the police no longer had a witness. The plan was to meet with Wild Apache and then have some dinner in New Kingston.

Anthony was behind the wheel of the Range Rover with Hernandez riding shotgun and Maria in the back. She was watching a movie on the DVD. Juan and his brother were in the Escalade with the other five women. They were stopped by the police doing a routine check at the bottom of Mountain View Avenue. Hernandez quickly dialed Mayweather's cell number. They didn't need any hassle from the cops right now. Everyone except the women was armed — plus the bit of recreational cocaine that the girls didn't leave home without. Mayweather answered as Anthony pulled over and rolled his window down.

The police were heavily armed and approached the vehicles warily with weapons drawn. Hernandez told Mayweather the situation and passed Anthony the phone.

"Any illegal firearms in this vehicle?" the officer asked gruffly, his rancid breath permeating the vehicle.

"Assistant Commissioner Mayweather is on the phone," Anthony said to the cop. "He wants to speak to the officer in charge." The cop looked at Anthony with distrust, smelling a trap. He trained his gun on Anthony and took the cell phone.

"Hello." He listened for a while, muttering a respectful 'Yes sir' at various intervals. He shoved the phone back to Anthony and waved them through. Anthony gave him a smirk and drove off. They arrived at Rockfort ten minutes later. This time Wild Apache had instructed them to just drive in; Anthony knew the way and the word was out that they were to be allowed through. Anthony pulled up at Wild Apache's house a few minutes later. They alighted from the vehicles and were met at the gate by two men armed with sub-machine guns. They greeted Hernandez and Anthony respectfully, nodded at Juan and Carlos, and leered at the women. Wild Apache was seated on his sofa dressed in jeans and a plaid shirt. The shirt was unbuttoned, showing off his bony chest and the chrome handgun tucked in his waist. He stood and shook Anthony's hand and was introduced to Hernandez.

"We finally meet face to face," Wild Apache said grinning; exposing teeth that badly needed the attention of a good dentist.

"Glad to be here," Hernandez responded.

Wild Apache gestured for the women and Juan and Carlos to make themselves at home, and gestured for Anthony and Hernandez to follow him out to the back veranda. His two trusted lieutenants, Reds and Scarface, were already seated out there, both smoking marijuana. They got down to business. Wild Apache and his crew were to go to the community known as Jungle and retrieve the sixteen kilos of cocaine that Benjie Dread had stashed at his base. Benjie Dread and his crew, the Rasta Rascals, were also to be killed. The community would then be taken over by Wild Apache and his crew. Wild Apache was pleased about this plan as Benjie Dread ran a lucrative extortion racket, preying on all the businesses in West Kingston. It was reputed to be a five million dollar a year racket. Not only would he be taking that over, but he would up the price. No one was immune to inflation. All Hernandez really wanted was the cocaine and the prospect of having more manpower at his disposal. The street soldiers in Jungle who survived the attack would be allowed to stay and be a part of the new regime. Those who refused would be executed. Hernandez had twenty kilos of cocaine on his yacht which was still docked in Port Royal. This sixteen would be added to it and shipped to Miami. Satisfied that everyone knew their role and were on the same page, Hernandez and his party departed.

"The bloodclaat Spanish gal dem look good eeh man," Wild Apache commented to Reds and Scarface after his guests had left. "When we kill Hernandez and him boys dem we ago bring all ah de girls dem inna de camp."

"Mi nuh think them can talk English," Reds responded, taking a deep drag of his marijuana spliff.

"That don't matter man, after ah nuh that we need them fah," Wild Apache retorted as they all laughed boisterously.

Hernandez puffed on his cigar as Anthony drove the luxurious vehicle at a moderate speed. He was pleased at how the meeting went. His stomach rumbled loudly.

"Where are we going for dinner?" He asked Anthony. "I want seafood."

"Well, we can go to Marva's on Ruthven Road," he replied, "Gavin told me they have the best seafood in Kingston."

"Good, step on it, *tengo hambre*," Hernandez said, thinking a nice lobster would do the trick.

Comemierda! Anthony thought inwardly, meeting Maria's gaze in the rear view mirror. Her eyes held laughter as if she read his mind. He wondered if she knew that he planned to kill Hernandez. He wondered if she wanted him to. Anthony couldn't think of any other reason why she would have told him about his mother. Though he had already made up his mind, he still loved Hernandez as a father. He had taken him in and shown him a life of opulence and excitement. For that he was grateful. But what he had done to Penelope was unforgivable. His mother had deserved better. Hernandez had to die; brutally. They pulled up at the Marva's several minutes later. It was a spacious, rooftop restaurant. The place was a bit packed so they were not able to sit at adjoining tables. Hernandez, Maria and Anthony sat at a table close to the entrance while Juan, his brother, and the other girls sat at another table close to the back. They all sipped on fish tea while they awaited their orders. Anthony felt someone's eyes on him. He turned around to see an attractive young woman staring at him, her eyes blazing with anger. Dana. She was at a table with a mature couple. Probably her parents; she resembled the woman. Anthony winked at her and turned back around. Obviously she was still pissed about the other night.

At six p.m. that evening, Wild Apache and his crew piled into two white, tinted Toyota Corollas. The cars were old and non-descript, but in good working condition — perfect for a mission of this nature. There were eight of them in total, four to a car. They were all dressed in fatigues and heavily armed. Wild Apache had his lucky feather in his pocket. An obeah woman had given it to him a year ago and he never went on a mission without it. They entered the community, and the car with Reds in it stopped a hundred yards from their destination, turned and parked. If reinforcements came when the gun fire erupted it would have to come from this direction. Benjie Dread's stash house was the last building on this cul-de-sac. The car with Wild Apache picked up speed and stopped suddenly in front of the base and three men alighted from the car quickly and immediately opened fire on the two Rastafarian men who were standing by the gate. They dropped like flies under the hail of bullets. They then rushed into the house with guns blazing. Three men who had been lounging in the living room watching football on TV had jumped up and grabbed their guns when they heard the sudden gun fire but they reacted too slowly. Only one of them managed to squeeze off two shots before they were all killed. His bullets had sailed harmlessly over the heads of the on-rushing men. Benjie Dread was in the back bedroom astride a young girl that he had sent for earlier, when he heard the chaos outside. She was only fifteen but that's how he liked them; young, ripe and tight. He jumped off the bed and foolishly attempted to put on his pants before reaching for his gun. His pants were halfway up when the door was kicked open.

"Don't move a muscle Rasta bwoy!" was the command from Wild Apache as he entered the room flanked by two of his henchmen. Benjie Dread didn't make a move for his gun which was lying on top of the bedside table but he continued to pull up his pants. Wild Apache stepped to him swiftly and hit him on the forehead with the butt of his AK 47. "Pussyhole, yuh nuh hear don't move!" He said harshly and kicked the Rastafarian in his stomach. The girl in the bed had balled up in a fetal position but was otherwise silent. Her eyes were wide as she watched the drama unfold. Wild Apache instructed Benjie Dread to take off his pants and stand naked with his hands on his head. Benjie cursed inwardly but did as he was told. How the rass those idiots outside had allowed themselves to be taken by surprise?

"Mi know say the coke deh yah, so tell me where yuh have it stash," Wild Apache said to him. Benjie Dread took too long to reply and was rewarded with a hard kick to his exposed genitals. He screamed and doubled over in pain. Wild Apache then grabbed a fistful of his locks and used his razor sharp combat knife to cut off a large chunk of Benjie's dirty, matted hair and stuffed it in his mouth. Benjie gagged and choked as he struggled to spit the hair out. He then kicked Benjie in the head and instructed the other two men to hurry and check the house. Wild Apache then looked the young girl in the eyes, grabbed Benjie Dread by the head and slit his throat. He grinned as the girl screamed when the blood from Benjie Dread splattered her.

"We find it boss," Scarface announced from the door way. Wild Apache decided to spare the girl's life so that she could spread his legend. He didn't fear her telling the cops. People in the ghetto hated and distrusted the police. He took Benjie Dread's 357 magnum and they hurried out with the two boxes filled with parcels of cocaine. They hopped into the waiting car and the lead vehicle which had been keeping watch further down the road sped off when they saw that their comrades were ready. A pickup truck with two Rastafarians in the cab and three crouched in the back with guns careened around the corner and turned sideways in the road, blocking the exit for the two oncoming vehicles. Wild Apache's driver pulled alongside the other car and they both stopped about two hundred yards from the pickup truck. They jumped from the vehicles and opened fire on the pickup truck, filling it with holes. The handguns the Rastafarians had were no match for the high powered rifles that Wild Apache's crew was carrying. The one in the passenger side got hit in his right arm and shoulder and they revved up the truck and beat a hasty retreat. One of the men fell from the back of the pick-up as it swerved erratically in their bid to escape the barrage of gunfire. Wild Apache's crew hopped back in their cars and the lead car ran the injured Rastafarian over as he tried to crawl out of the road. The pickup truck was nowhere to be seen as they quickly drove out of the neighbourhood. People scampered out in the road talking excitedly at what they had just witnessed from the cover of their homes. Benjie Dread's time had expired; a new don would be taking over.

Terri had slept for a couple hours after chatting with Anna on the phone. Anna had teased her mercilessly about her tryst with Anthony. Now she was on her way to Waterloo Avenue to see if any of the prostitutes had ventured out yet. She hoped one of them would be able to give her some information. Terri groaned as she drove down Constant Spring Road. Her parents had invited her over for Sunday dinner and she had overeaten. A hefty portion of her Mom's delicious sweet-potato pie was now wrecking havoc with her stomach. She promised herself to work it off tomorrow. There were about four prostitutes out when she turned onto Waterloo Avenue. The early bird catches the worm, Terri thought as she pulled over to the curb and got out of the car.

"Yes pretty girl, yuh come to the right place," said a rather young looking girl, as she approached Terri with a sexy strut.

Terri leaned against the car. "Are you soliciting an officer of the law young lady?"

The girl frowned and then her eyes widened. "Jesus Christ! Sorry miss, mi never see say ah you. Mi see yuh on TV all the time. No disrespect."

"How old are you?"

"Nineteen," the girl stated proudly.

Terri shook her head. "I need to ask you a few questions. Were you out here last night?"

"Yes."

"Do you know this woman?" Terri asked, showing her a passport size photograph of the murdered prostitute.

"Yes, mi know her," the girl said nodding. "She love gwaan like she nice."

"Did you see her last night?"

"Yeah, she did goweh with somebody in a black Escalade."

"Did you get a look at the driver?"

"No the windows did tint," the girl replied, adding, "Mi hear say she get murda. Is true officer?"

"Yes, she was killed last night," Terri responded.

"Mi neva like her but mi sorry fi hear still. It coulda happen to any one of us. It dangerous pon de road but money haffi make," the girl reasoned.

Terri thanked her for her help and drove off. Her cell phone rang as she turned onto Trafalgar Road. The name on her caller ID put a smile on her face.

"Hi Tony," she said.

"Hey sexy," Anthony intoned. He had just polished off a huge steamed fish served with lots of okra and bammy.

"What are you up to?" Terri asked.

"Nothing much. Finished up some business and had dinner with my uncle and associates," Anthony replied. "I'm hoping to see you later so I can have dessert."

Terri blushed. Just the thought of having him inside her made her face glow. The man was addictive. "Hope you're not diabetic, my dessert is really sweet..." Terri teased. Anthony laughed and told her he would swing by about ten. Anthony hung up the phone and looked at his reflection in the mirror. He was inside the rest room of the restaurant. He really liked Terri but a man in his line of work couldn't afford the distraction of falling in love — especially with the enemy. Unfortunately she was already under his skin. He went back out front to rejoin the others. The seven o' clock news was on the TV mounted in the corner close to their table. The reporter was on location in the community of Arnett Gardens, popularly known as Jungle. He was reporting that there had been a shootout between rival gangs resulting in the slaying of seven men; one of whom was area don Benjie Dread. Hernandez grinned and toasted Anthony. As if on cue, Hernandez's cell phone rang. It was Wild Apache.

"Everything cool, mi have the merchandise," Wild Apache said without preamble.

"Good job," Hernandez responded, "I'll pick it up on my way out to the yacht tomorrow."

"Alright, jus' call me when you coming," Wild Apache said and ended the call.

Hernandez then placed an overseas call to Miami. He let his associate know that a shipment of thirty-six kilos of cocaine would be coming in later that week.

Terri pulled up at police headquarters and parked in her spot. Mayweather's ugly, green gas guzzler was not on the premises. Great, Terri thought. She was hoping not to run into him today. She waved hi to the receptionist and the few officers in the lobby and boarded the elevator. Her office was on the fourth floor along with the offices of the Commissioner and the Assistant Commissioner — much to Mayweather's chagrin. He had been furious when the Commissioner gave her this office last year. Terri wondered how his wife tolerated him. She was such a nice, pleasant lady; though she hadn't seen her since she quit her administrative job at headquarters a few years ago. Terri entered her comfortable office and closed the door behind her. The office was dominated by a large mahogany desk which was neatly kept. Her state-of-the-art laptop, a family photo of her and her parents and a penholder with a clock were the only things on her desk. All paperwork was kept hidden away in her desk drawers which she kept locked at all times. The wall behind her was filled with her academic and professional accomplishments.

Terri pulled the files on the current murder case and started working. She planned to stay there for at least three hours then go home and give Anthony his dessert.

Anthony and the crew noisily exited the restaurant at a few minutes to eight. Hernandez was telling one of his stories and everyone except Anthony laughed dutifully. When they reached the bottom of the stairs there was a striking woman on her way upstairs. She was with a well-built, cocky looking man who had his arm draped possessively around her shoulder. Anthony recognized her immediately. It was Terri's friend.

"Hi," Anna said pleasantly, "We never formally met. I'm Anna."

"Nice to meet you, I'm Tony," Anthony replied.

"This is my boyfriend Raymond," Anna announced, introducing the guy to Anthony. The men nodded at each other.

"Well, good to see you, take care Tony," Anna said and proceeded to go upstairs.

Anthony caught up with the others who had gone ahead to the parking lot. When Anna and Raymond were settled at their table she dialed Terri's cell.

"Hey girl, guess who I just ran into?" Anna said when Terri came on the line.

"Who?"

"Your Latin lover," Anna teased. "I'm at Marva's with Raymond."

"Ok, he told me he was having dinner there," Terri replied. "I'm supposed to be seeing him later."

"Good for you," Anna said, "Talk to you later."

"Bye." Terri checked the time and immediately settled back down to work.

"You've been kinda pensive lately Tony," Hernandez remarked on the ride back to the mansion. "Everything ok?"

"Yeah Padre," Anthony replied easily. "I'm good."

"Good," Hernandez responded, adding, "Tomorrow we'll pick up the coke from Wild Apache and take it out to the yacht. We can go for a little sailing."

"Ok, we can leave out about eleven in the morning," Anthony said as he turned on Stony Hill road.

"Yeah, that's a good time," Hernandez agreed. He reclined in his seat and wondered what was bugging Anthony. He wasn't buying it for fifty cents that everything was ok. He had known Anthony for twelve years and knew when something was wrong. Besides, a man didn't get as far as he did in this business by taking people at face value. He would keep a close eye on Tony for the next couple days. One can never be too careful. They arrived home fifteen minutes later. Hernandez and Maria went to their room and he got into bed and instructed Maria to put on her maid costume. He felt like a bit of role playing tonight. The others went out to the pool where they all got naked and proceeded to have an orgy. Anthony went to his room and stripped down to his boxers.

He did calisthenics for half an hour and took a long, cold shower. He felt refreshed and invigorated. He couldn't wait to go see Terri.

Terri got home at nine-thirty and prepared a bubble bath. She listened to R&B star Usher confess his sins as she soaked the day away. She shaved the bit of new growth on her legs and vagina and finished up her bath. Terri then rummaged through her lingerie drawer for her sheer red lacy number. Anthony's eyes were guaranteed to pop out of his head when he sees me in this she thought confidently. She hadn't gotten a chance to wear it for anyone since she purchased it a few months ago. She was alerted at two minutes to ten by the security guard at the gate that she had a visitor. Anthony parked behind Terri's car and the front door swung open just as he was getting ready to ring the doorbell. Anthony gasped audibly when he looked at Terri. She looked absolutely stunning. Her long, wavy hair cascaded down past her shoulders, stopping to rest just above the nipples of her ample breasts. Her nipples were erect and straining against the lacy material. Her curvy, supple body looked delicious through the sheer fabric. Her smile was provocative and her eyes were alive with lust and anticipation. Anthony felt as if all the blood in his body had flowed to his dick. It was so hard it felt painful. He closed the door behind him and pounced on Terri. They didn't make it to the bedroom. Anthony took her on the carpet, over the arm of the couch, against the living room wall and finally on the kitchen counter. Their coupling was frenzied and passionate. Forty-five minutes later, they lay spent in Terri's queen size bed cooling off with the air conditioner on full blast.

"That was really intense," Anthony remarked, as Terri traced the outline of the huge tattoo on his chest.

"It's kinda scary how free I am sexually with you." She looked up in his face. "You make me feel so alive."

"What's really happening with us Terri?" Anthony asked as he played with her hair.

"I don't know Tony...I mean I smile when I hear your voice on the phone...I think about you an indecent amount of times daily... and we haven't even known each other for a week. It just dosen't make any sense...how can I be so connected to you in such a short space of time?"

"Shhh…" Anthony put a finger to her lips. Terri took it in her mouth. Anthony moaned and pulled her onto him. She was still incredibly wet so he slid inside her easily.

"Ohhh…Tony you need to put on a condom…," Terri breathed as she rode him slowly.

"Yeah….," Anthony moaned in agreement as he savored the incredible feeling of being inside her unsheathed.

Terri quickened her pace and threw her head back. "Don't come inside me ok..," she said as she clenched and unclenched her vaginal muscles, eliciting some loud grunts from Anthony. Terri then rotated while he was still embedded in her and put her back to him. Anthony lost control at the sight of her ass bouncing up and down rapidly. He gripped her hips tightly and bucked upwards uncontrollably.

"I'm about to come Terri," he warned, his eyes tightly closed as his body succumbed to the sensations it was feeling.

"Wet me up Tony…splash off inside me," Terri said wantonly, surprising her own ears. Anthony groaned loudly and trembled as he emptied his seed. She sat astride him until he lost his erection and slipped out.

"I can't believe I just did that," Terri said. "That was very irresponsible…"

"Relax, Terri," Anthony said soothingly. "You can take a morning-after pill tomorrow. Besides…we would make some really cute babies." He grinned at her.

"Tony don't joke about this," Terri frowned. Then she smiled at him. "We would though wouldn't we…"

"I'll be sure to stop at the pharmacy tomorrow on my way to the office," she told him, now serious. "I don't plan to have any children out of wedlock."

Anthony didn't respond. What the fuck am I going to do, he pondered as he looked at Terri, who was now snuggled up against him, her head resting on his chest. I've never loved a woman so I'm not sure what I'm feeling. But it's so intense.

Terri woke up a few hours later and checked the time. It was two a.m. Anthony was fast asleep. He looks so innocent, Terri thought, as she quietly got up out of the bed. He didn't stir. She slipped on her robe and went out to the kitchen to get some juice. She drank a glass of fruit punch and went into the living room to turn off the lights. It didn't seem as if

Anthony would be leaving tonight. She picked up the scattered clothing from their earlier romp in the living room. His keys fell out his pocket as she picked up his pants. She picked them up and noticed it was for a Cadillac Escalade.

Surprised, she looked out the window. The moonlight was bright and she saw the shiny, black Escalade parked behind her car. She noticed she was breathing heavily and forced herself to relax. A brown man in a black Escalade the little boy had told her. Stop being silly Terri, she chided herself, don't jump to conclusions. She felt his wallet in his back pocket and tried to resist the urge to look in it. She couldn't. Terri sat on the sofa and removed the wallet. It was thick and expensive. Gucci. It was full of money. She counted eighteen hundred US dollars. There were two credit cards; a platinum Master card and a Visa. They were not in his name. Gavin L. Wilkinson. Terri frowned. She knew Wilkinson. Hot shot defense attorney. He had recently defended a known murderer and gotten him off on a technicality. She had been furious at the verdict, wishing that she had shot the perpetrator instead of arresting him. At least then justice would have been served. What was Anthony doing with his credit cards? Terri continued to check the wallet. She found two drivers licenses. One Cuban, the other Jamaican. There was nothing else in the wallet except for a photograph. It was of Anthony and an older Hispanic man, lounging at a table drinking champagne and surrounded by beautiful women.

Terri wondered what to make of what she had discovered. But what had she actually discovered? He was a businessman, though it was strange to be carrying around so much cash and credit cards that were not in his name. It had to be a coincidence that he matched the ID of the man the little boy had told her about. Having two drivers' licenses was not illegal. Well, one thing was certain; her initial perception of Anthony was on the ball. There was definitely more to him than met the eye. Terri put the wallet back in Anthony's back pocket and took up his shirt and loafers and took them to the bedroom where she placed them in her closet. Anthony awakened when she got back into bed and immediately reached for her. She melted in his arms, her discomfort temporarily forgotten.

CHAPTER 7

Anthony woke up at five the next morning. He gently shook Terri awake.

"Hmm..," she murmured sleepily. The room was now cold as the air conditioning had been left on all night.

"Baby, I gotta go," he told her softly.

"What time is it?" she asked, her eyes still closed.

"Its five a.m."

"Your clothes are in the closet," she told him, as she sat up and reached for the remote to turn off the air conditioner. Anthony got up and went to the closet to retrieve his clothes.

"Would you like some breakfast?" Terri asked through a yawn.

"No baby, no need to bother yourself," Anthony replied as he tugged on his trousers. He went into the bathroom, peed and washed his face. Terri slipped on her robe and walked him to the door.

"I'll call you later." He kissed her softly and left the house. He started the SUV and took his gun and cell phone from the glove compartment. He checked his phone and saw that he had two missed calls. Both from Hernandez. The last call was at twelve-thirty last night. Fuck is he checking up on me for, Anthony thought irritably. He put the phone down and drove off. The security guard let him through with a wave.

Terri went back to bed and snuggled up with her pillows. She could smell Anthony's scent on her sheets. Unable to go back to sleep, she turned on the TV and put it on CNN. As she watched the latest developments on the situation in Iraq, her mind drifted to Tony. She wondered if he got home okay, then it occurred to her that she didn't even know where he was staying. He also hadn't introduced her

66

to his uncle. She decided not to pressure him but if he didn't take her to his house soon she would ask him about it.

Everyone was still asleep when Anthony arrived at the mansion ten minutes later. He took a quick hot shower and went into his bedroom. Thankfully his bed was empty. After three intense rounds with Terri last night he was completely worn out. He immediately fell asleep.

Terri went straight to Horizon Wireless after she left home at eight a.m. She was anxious to get her hands on Barry Laylor's phone records. The manager had promised her the information first thing that morning. She had also given him Laylor's cell phone to see if one of his technicians could unlock his phonebook. She was smartly dressed in a fitted navy blue pinstripe pantsuit. Her hair was pulled back tightly in a bun and her face was adorned with Chanel sunglasses. She looked more like a highly successful business executive than a detective. She arrived there at eight thirty and advised the receptionist that she was there to see Mr. Carson. She was immediately ushered into his office and after a few minutes of politely listening to his many compliments, she left with a package containing the information she needed.

Terri joined the steady stream of Monday morning traffic and headed to Police headquarters. She got there thirty minutes later. She had a brief meeting with the lead detective handling the murders that had occurred in Jungle on Sunday night and then she went to her office, advising the secretary that she was not to be disturbed for the next hour. Terri opened the package and removed the contents. There were two stacks of papers; one for his office land line and the other for his cell phone. There was also Laylor's cell phone for which the phonebook had been successfully unlocked. Terri checked his phonebook first. Gavin Wilkinson. Hmmm, Gavin seems to be Mr. Popular, Terri thought, first his name pops up in Anthony's wallet and now Laylor's cell phone. She planned to meet with Wilkinson real soon. Have a chat with him. The egotistical bastard loved to talk. She might learn something useful. Pablo Hernandez. An overseas number. She checked the area code. Cuba. Terri checked Laylor's received calls option on his cell phone. This man had called him twice on the day before he was killed. She went back into the phonebook and scrolled down. Claude Mayweather. He had Mayweather's cell number and home number. Mayweather had given no indication that he knew the man personally. Terri checked the stacks of paper to see how often Laylor spoke with Mayweather. The print out of his cell phone call records indicate that he had called Mayweather everyday for the last three days leading up to his death. He also had called that Cuban number quite a few times for the entire month. Terri scrolled through the phonebook. She recognized some more of the names. A few prominent businessmen; a popular female recording artiste; a Government Minister; Anna Evans. My god, Terri thought. If Anna had slept with Barry Laylor that was a new low, even for her. She would ask her about it later.

Terri buzzed the secretary on the intercom and instructed her to call Gavin Wilkinson's office and get him on the phone. She buzzed Terri four minutes later to say that he was on the line.

"Mr. Wilkinson, good day sir," Terri said.

"To what do I owe this pleasure," Wilkinson responded.

"Is it possible for us to meet this evening? I think you might be able to assist me with an investigation."

Wilkinson thought for a moment. Guess it wouldn't hurt to meet with the gorgeous detective. "Sure. On one condition…."

"What's that?"

"That we meet over dinner." Gavin checked the time as he waited for her response.

"I'll meet you at six at Marva's," Terri replied. The things I do for justice she thought.

"Great. See you then." Gavin then grabbed his jacket and headed out the door. He was running late for an appointment.

Anthony got up at ten that morning. He took a shower, got dressed and went downstairs. Hernandez was watching sports highlights on ESPN. Three of the girls were thumbing through fashion magazines. The other two were playing cards with Juan and Carlos, and Maria was in the kitchen having some cereal.

"Hey Padre," Anthony said as he went to join Maria at the kitchen counter.

"I called you a couple times last night Tony." He sounded annoyed. "It's not like you to just up and disappear like that. Where were you?"

"I went to visit someone," Anthony replied, adding in a sarcastic tone, "Next time I'll ask your permission."

"Tony I love like a son but you better watch your fucking mouth!" Hernandez exploded. "You've been acting really weird lately. You better get your act together real soon." His tone was ominous.

Anthony looked at him calmly. "Are you threatening me padre?"

The tension in the room was thick as both men stared at each other. Juan and Carlos fidgeted nervously, unsure of what to do. Their job was to protect Hernandez — against anyone.

Hernandez held his gaze for a moment. Then he smiled. "Look at us. Arguing like females. You're like a son to me Tony. I'm just worried about you. That's all."

"It's ok, Padre. No big deal," Anthony replied. The tension slowly dissipated but both knew that things would never be the same between them after this incident. Juan and Carlos breathed easy and resumed their card game. Maria continued to eat her cereal. She already knew that it was just a matter of time before Anthony killed Hernandez but after what just happened, she saw it in Hernandez's eyes that he was going to have Anthony killed.

"Ok let's roll out," Hernandez announced and led the way outside. Maria and Anthony were the last ones out. Maria looked at him. Her eyes told him she would help him if he needed it. He nodded and they joined the others outside. They piled into the Escalade and Anthony drove out. Hernandez called Wild Apache to let him know that they were on their way. Anthony's stomach rumbled as he turned into the Rockfort community. He was famished. They pulled up at Wild Apache's gate a few minutes later. Hernandez and Anthony went inside to see him while the others remained in the vehicle. Wild Apache met them on the verandah and ushered them inside. Hernandez immediately got down to business.

"Where's the coke?" He asked, after they had greeted each other.

Wild Apache gestured at two boxes that were on the floor next to the coffee-table. Anthony checked the boxes. He frowned. "This is only ten kilos. We were told that they had sixteen."

"Well, yuh information did wrong then," Wild Apache responded. "Dat is all they had."

Hernandez's eyes narrowed. He was sure Wild Apache was holding out on him.

"We going out to the yacht to do a little sailing and partying with the girls. You want to join us?"

Wild Apache grinned. "Yeah man! Dat sound good. Reds and Scarface haffi come wid mi though."

"No problem," Hernandez responded. He shouted for Juan and Carlos to come and load the boxes in the trunk of the SUV. Wild Apache then called for Reds and Scarface who were in the den smoking weed and they got into Wild Apache's Honda Accord and drove out behind the Escalade.

"Can't believe the nerve of that scrawny Indian," Hernandez remarked to Anthony as they drove out to the harbour. "Trying to rob me. Greedy bastard."

Anthony grunted in response. As far as he was concerned, killing Wild Apache would be a pleasure. He never liked him from day one.

"Yuh feel say dem believe yuh bout the coke?" Reds queried from his perch on the backseat.

Wild Apache met his eyes in the rearview mirror. "If him nuh believe mi dat a fi him business. What him can do bout it? Ah we do the work so we fi get some of the coke."

Reds nodded in agreement. If one of them even blinked wrong he wouldn't hesitate to light them up. He caressed the large handgun in his lap lovingly.

"Ah hope we get fi fuck a couple ah de gal dem," Scarface commented. "Mi neva fuck a foreign gal yet."

"Yeah man, dat haffi gwaan," Wild Apache said, taking a deep drag of the spliff that Scarface handed to him. "Fi real."

They reached the harbour twenty minutes later. They parked and everyone alighted from the vehicles. Wild Apache was impressed when he saw the yacht.

"Yuh boat look good man," he said to Hernandez as they walked to the deck.

"Thanks," Hernandez responded. The crew of three that were staying on the yacht had prepared a huge feast of peppered shrimp, fried fish, fritatas and rice and beans. Champagne and coronas were on ice. Hernandez told his guests to relax and make themselves at home. Juan and Carlos took the cocaine below deck and returned in beach shorts. The girls were already in bikinis. Anthony dug into the food with gusto as the yacht set sail. The plan was to sail to Negril on the island's west end. Hernandez wanted to check out a beach front property that Gavin Wilkinson had told him was up for sale. Wild Apache and his boys availed themselves of the food and drink as they relaxed on deck. It was the first time either of them had been on a yacht. Salsa music blared from the speakers. One of the girls gestured for Wild Apache to come and dance with her. Wild Apache grinned and accepted her invitation. Reds and Scarface laughed boisterously as they watched their boss try to do the meringue. Their laughter turned to lust when the girl led Wild Apache by the hand downstairs. Two of the other girls came over to where they were sitting and started dancing sensuously with each other. The men grinned as they feasted their eyes on the two voluptuous gyrating beauties.

Wild Apache followed the girl into one of the rooms below deck. She led him over to the bunk bed and knelt down in front him. He eagerly removed his gun from his waist and unbuckled his jeans. He moaned loudly as she took his small erect penis in her mouth. He closed his eyes as he enjoyed the best blowjob of his life. Anthony opened the door quietly and slipped into the room.

"Bloodclaat...don't stop," Wild Apache groaned as he began to move his bony hips in a circular motion.

"Hey gal..." he began and opened his eyes when she abruptly stopped. His eyes were wide as he stared at the gun in Anthony's hand. The girl took Wild Apache's gun from off the bed and passed it to Anthony. He stuck it in his waist with his free hand.

"A whe yuh a do rude bwoy?" Wild Apache asked nervously, beads of perspiration breaking out on his forehead and upper lip.

"Where's the rest of the coke and the money we paid you to do the job?" Anthony asked.

"Everything deh at the ho...house," Wild Apache stammered. "Mi neva mean fi..."

"Where in the house?" Anthony demanded, cutting him off in mid-sentence.

"Inna de room beside the back veranda," Wild Apache said. "Duh mi ah beg..."

Anthony shot him in the face, killing him instantly. He pressed a buzzer and two of the crew members came into the room and put Wild Apache's body in a bag and began to clean up the mess. Anthony instructed the girl to stay below deck and went back upstairs. He nodded discreetly to Hernandez as he poured himself a glass of champagne.

The girls were now seated on the laps of Reds and Scarface, giggling and caressing their arms and chests. The one sitting on Scarface's lap licked his ear and got up, extending her hand. Scarface took her hand excitedly and eagerly followed her downstairs. She opened the door to one of the rooms and they stepped in. The room was pitch black.

"Turn on de light," Scarface instructed, breathing heavily. "Mi want fi see yuh body."

She obliged him and switched the light on, moving away from him quickly as she did so. Scarface cursed and tried to pull his gun as Juan and Carlos pounced on him, inflicting multiple stab wounds all over his body. He finally stopped struggling when he was stabbed in the heart.

Upstairs on deck, Anthony walked over to where Reds was sitting with the girl in his lap. He refilled Reds' glass with champagne.

"Enjoying yourself?" Anthony asked.

"Yeah man," Reds replied.

Anthony then suddenly threw the contents of his glass into Reds' face and cracked him over the head with the champagne bottle. The girl jumped off his lap as he staggered off the chair, dazed but still conscious. Anthony moved to him swiftly and stabbed him in his right eye with the piece of broken bottle that was still in his hand. Reds screamed and remarkably tried to reach for his gun. Anthony admired his resilience. He kicked Reds in the scrotum and kicked his head back when he doubled over in pain. Reds fell on his back and Anthony placed a foot on his neck and pumped six shots in his stomach. Hernandez and Maria watched from their perch where he was reclined on a lounge chair, shirtless with Maria lightly rubbing his shoulders.

Anthony walked over to them. "I have his car keys. The car is tinted so no one in the community will realize that they are not the ones in the car. I know exactly where the money and the coke are in the house."

"Good job Tony," Hernandez said sincerely. It was unfortunate that he would have to kill Tony but that's the nature of this business. Anthony seemed to have ambitions of being the boss. That could be the only reason why he was acting so weird and openly challenging his authority. "We'll go up there when we get back from Negril."

They watched as two of the crew members placed Reds' body in a bag and clean up the mess on the deck. "Instruct them to tie weights to the bags and throw them overboard on the way back from Negril," Hernandez said to Anthony as he went below deck with Maria. He felt for a quickie. Anthony whipped out his cell phone and called Terri.

"Hi Tony."

"Hi baby, how's your day?" he asked, as he lit a cigar and enjoyed the scenery.

"Very busy and productive. What are you up to?" Her stomach rumbled, reminding her that she hadn't eaten lunch.

"I'm on my way to Negril with my Uncle. We have some property to check out," he replied.

"Really, that's a long drive. How far have you reached?"

Anthony paused momentarily. "I think we're in St. Elizabeth."

Terri chuckled. "You still have a long way to go. Be careful. I miss you."

"I miss you too *amante.*"

"Later baby."

"Bye." Anthony sighed. He hoped she hadn't taken the morning-after pill. He had wanted to ask but didn't want to raise it just in case she had forgotten. He doubted that she would forget though. He went below deck to change. They were approaching Negril and he had specks of blood on his shirt.

Terri called Anna to find out if she was free for lunch. She was. They met at a popular Chinese restaurant in New Kingston. Anna got there before Terri as she had just completed a photo shoot at a hotel close by.

"Hey girl," Anna said as they hugged.

"I'm starving," Terri said as she picked up the menu. She ordered sweet and sour chicken with shrimp fried rice while Anna ordered chow mein.

"The photographer at the shoot was such an ass. The shoot was supposed to take two hours but dragged on for three and a half."

"Anna," Terri said, "Were you friends with Barry Laylor?"

"Why do you ask?" Anna said, surprised at the question.

"I saw your number in his cell phone." They were quiet as the waiter gave them their order.

"Yeah, I slept with him once or twice a few months ago," Anna said nonchalantly when the waiter left.

"Goodness Anna," Terri exclaimed, "What could possess you to sleep with that obese man?"

"He's a powerful businessman Terri," Anna said matter-of-factly. "Sometimes sex has nothing to do with looks."

Terri shook her head and took a bite of her chicken.

"T, after all these years you want to start judging me?" Anna demanded.

"I'm not judging you An," Terri said soothingly. "I was just surprised that's all."

"I love you Beatrice," Terri added, grinning. Beatrice was Anna's middle name which she hated dearly.

She smirked at Terri and then laughed. "I love you too girl."

The awkward moment passed and the two old friends ate lunch while Anna grilled Terri about her budding romance with Anthony.

The yacht arrived at the mariner in Negril at two thirty that afternoon. Hernandez called the owner for the property and he sent a driver to pick up Hernandez. Anthony and Maria accompanied him while the others stayed on board. The property was a ten minute drive from the mariner. The owner was a tall, skinny half-German man. He greeted them and gave them a tour of the property. It was six acres of prime beachfront property. It housed a lovely seven bedroom villa. Hernandez loved it. He shook hands with the man and told him his lawyer would be in touch with him tomorrow to close the deal. He offered them something to drink to celebrate but Hernandez declined, telling him he had urgent matters to attend to back in Kingston. The driver took them back to the mariner and they set sail back to Kingston. The crew members attached weights to the body bags and dumped the three bodies overboard about thirty miles from Negril.

CHAPTER 8

Afghan lunch with Anna, Terri went back to the office at two p.m. She met with a woman who had witnessed a murder and was willing to testify in court. Terri got the paperwork in motion for the woman to be placed in the witness protection program. The program was relatively new to Jamaica. Terri had been instrumental in getting the program implemented two years ago. Sadly, the majority of Jamaicans had little faith in the program due to the public perception of the police force. It was deemed to be highly corrupt and people did not feel safe entrusting them with their lives. Terri sighed as she thought of her suspicions regarding Mayweather. If it indeed turns out that he was somehow mixed up in the killings of Barry Laylor and the security guard, the shit would really hit the fan. The Assistant Commissioner of Police involved in murder? The press would have a field day. Terri hoped it wouldn't get to that but her gut feeling told her otherwise. She checked the time. She had a meeting with Mayweather and two junior detectives in an hour.

Elaine Mayweather was in the kitchen cooking dinner when the gardener knocked on the kitchen door. Elaine opened the door. He was young, about twenty five and looked strong and muscular. He was clean cut and had a nice smile.

"Howdy Miss," he said smiling. "Ah just troubling you for a drink of cold water."

"Sure, Howard," she replied. "Are you almost finished?" She handed him a tall glass of water.

"Yes Miss." He drank the water thirstily. "Just need to rake up the section by the garage and then that's it."

Elaine looked at him as he drank. He was sweaty and his muscles glistened in his tank top. His worn jeans were close fitting and her eyes strayed to his crotch. She was so deep in thought that she didn't realize he was talking to her.

"Miss...you okay?" he asked, looking at her quizzically.

"Huh...yes I'm fine," she said quickly. She took the glass from his outstretched hand and placed it in the sink.

"I like that hairstyle Miss," he told her. "Makes you look a lot younger if you don't mind me saying so."

"Thank you Howard," Elaine said. She had cut her hair two days ago in a nice cropped style to cheer herself up after the last horrific encounter with her husband. This was the first compliment she had received from a man in God knows how long. "That's very kind of you."

"Alright then Miss, I'm going to finish up." He turned and walked away.

Elaine sighed and closed the door. That little interaction with the gardener had driven home the fact that she was a lonely middle-aged woman who was badly in need of some male affection. For better or for worse, she had said at the altar. For the past six years things had gotten progressively worse. She was now absolutely terrified of her husband. She never knew what to expect when he got angry these days. She knew one thing though, the abuse had to stop. She tasted the stew peas and added a bit more salt. She would let it simmer for ten more minutes and then she would have dinner. Just in time to relax and watch her favourite soap opera.

Terri knocked on Mayweather's office door promptly at four.

"Come in," came his gravelly baritone from inside the office.

"Good evening, sir," she said as she took a seat across from him. "I thought the two junior detectives would be a part of this meeting."

"No need, they have sent up a written report," Mayweather replied as he looked at her with undisguised lust. Terri groaned inwardly. His nasty ass simply wanted to meet with her alone.

"Ok, where do we start?" Terri asked, wanting to get the briefing over with as soon as possible. For the next fifteen minutes she eloquently bought him up to date on outstanding matters. She withheld certain bits of information as she didn't want him to have any idea that she was suspicious of him.

"So how you doing in general?" he said to her, as she gathered her papers together and prepared to leave.

"I'm doing just fine, sir," she replied politely. "Enjoy the rest of your evening."

"Have a drink with me before you leave detective," He offered, rising from his seat and going to the trolley that was laden with alcoholic beverages. Terri was surprised as he hadn't tried that tactic in awhile.

"No, thank you, sir," she said firmly as she turned to leave.

"You think your shit can make patty detective? Why you always acting so high and mighty?" Mayweather demanded angrily.

Terri was taken aback at the venom in his tone. She did not respond and hurriedly left his office, slamming the door behind her. She sat behind her desk and took a deep breath. She didn't think she could continue to work with Mayweather. The man was incorrigible.

Mayweather angrily poured himself a shot of whiskey. That fucking bitch, he fumed. He was angry with her for not being interested in him and he was even angrier with himself for the effect that she had on him. He felt like he would go crazy if he never got a chance to fuck her. He downed his whiskey and smiled cruelly. He would rape her. Yeah, that's it. She would never report it. He had an erection as he thought of the best way to carry out the act.

Terri left the office at five-thirty to meet Gavin Wilkinson at Marva's. The traffic was heavy and she didn't get there until six-fifteen. Terri looked around. He hadn't arrived yet. She got a corner table for two and ordered fish tea. Gavin strolled in fifteen minutes later. He looked sloppy in an ill-fitting brown suit. He spotted her and grinned. He walked over to the table and plopped down opposite Terri.

"Sorry I'm late detective," He apologized. "The traffic was ridiculous."

"That's fine, I totally understand," Terri responded.

"What are you having?" He asked as he gestured for a waiter.

"I'm fine. I just had some fish tea. I'm not really hungry."

"Nonsense, you can't possibly just sit there and watch me eat," he protested. "Try the steam fish. They have the best steam fish in Kingston."

"No, really, I'm fine," Terri said firmly.

"Suit yourself," he said testily. "Let me have the steam fish with bammy."

The waiter took his order and left. He leaned back in his chair and clasped his hands. "So, how can I help you detective?"

Terri was about to respond when Wilkinson's cell phone rang. He looked at the caller ID and gestured to Terri that he had to take the call.

"Pablo, what's up?" He said gaily. He watched Terri as he listened to his caller.

"Ok, good. I told you that you would like it. Negril is nice man." Terri listened intently while she pretended to look bored and examine her nails.

"Alright, I'll get the paperwork ready tomorrow. Hail up Tony for me."

"Yeah, bye." He slipped the cell phone back in his jacket. "Ok, I'm all yours," he grinned.

Terri did not return his smile. "What was your relationship with Barry Laylor?"

"Who says I had a relationship with him?" He replied.

"Are you denying that you knew the man?"

"Barry was an acquaintance of mine. We moved in the same circles," Wilkinson replied, adding sarcastically, "Am I a suspect?"

"Not yet," Terri shot back. "When was the last time you had any contact with him?"

"I really can't remember, we didn't speak often." The waiter arrived with his order. The food smelled delicious but Terri had no appetite. Her mind was swirling. She didn't believe in too many coincidences. Wilkinson had referred to the man who called him as Pablo. Pablo was also a name in Laylor's phonebook. Pablo Hernandez. She had to find out if it was the same man. But how? She couldn't just ask Gavin.

"You seemed really excited by that call," Terri said casually, giving him her most winning smile. "You closed a big deal?"

"Well, a client of mine went to look at some property in Negril today and decided to purchase it. There's a nice commission in it for me." He grinned at Terri.

More coincidences. Wilkinson had told the man to 'hail up Tony'. His client went to Negril today to look at property. Anthony and his uncle went to Negril today for the same purpose. Was this Pablo the same Pablo Hernandez in Laylor's phonebook? Was he Anthony's uncle?

"Your client must be a wealthy man. Real estate prices in Negril are through the roof," Terri commented.

Wilkinson removed a fish bone from his mouth. "Yep, he's filthy rich. Besides, he's a foreigner so he has an advantage with the foreign exchange rate."

Bingo. It must be the same man. Terri decided not to press him further.

"Do you know of any enemies Laylor might have had?" she asked.

"No, can't think of anyone who would want him dead," Gavin responded as he drank some soda and belched loudly.

Terri was appalled at his disgusting behaviour. No class. There are just some things money can't buy. "Well, thank you very much for meeting with me." Terri told him.

"Sorry I couldn't be of more help," Gavin said as he brushed bammy crumbs off his tie and shirt.

Oh you've been very helpful Terri thought inwardly. Aloud she said, "Enjoy the rest of your evening."

"It doesn't have to end now, wanna go have a drink?" Gavin asked hopefully.

"No, thank you," Terri replied, standing up. "I have to get back to the office."

"Ok, maybe some other time. See you around detective." Terri waved goodbye as Gavin reached for his cell phone to take a call.

Terri exited the restaurant deep in thought. She needed to find out exactly who this Pablo Hernandez character is. She would call her contacts at Immigration to find out if they had any information on him. The Commissioner was due back in the island tomorrow. She needed to speak with him. She wanted to tap Gavin Wilkinson's phone and only he could authorize it. Problem is she would have to explain to him why Mayweather had to be left out of the loop. Her suspicions about Mayweather were circumstantial at best; convincing the Commissioner that his deputy was involved in murder without concrete evidence would be a monumental task. She was banking on the fact that he had the utmost respect for her and her analytical skills. The yacht got back to the harbour in Port Royal at six-thirty p.m. Anthony outlined to Hernandez, Juan and Carlos how they were going to retrieve the cocaine and money from Wild Apache's house. It was a dangerous task as there were sure to be armed men at the house and there was only one way in and way out of the community. They had to be quick and decisive. They retrieved some bigger weapons from the yacht and Anthony hopped into Wild Apache's Honda Accord, with Carlos riding shotgun. Juan hopped behind the wheel of the Escalade and they headed out. Anthony was thankful that the car was tinted. That would make things much easier as everyone would assume that it was Wild Apache behind the wheel. The two vehicles turned into the Rockfort community thirty minutes later. Several times along the way, various people on the roadside waved to the car thinking it was Wild Apache. Anthony blew the horn to acknowledge them. When they arrived at the house, Anthony parked Wild Apache's car and hopped out quickly with two handguns, while Juan spun the Escalade around and stopped it at the gate, hopping out leaving the engine running. Hernandez remained in the vehicle, holding a pump rifle in his hand.

Anthony then quickly led the way into the yard. A man who Anthony recognized as Wild Apache's cousin came out to the veranda. Anthony shot him immediately in the head. He stepped over the dead body and entered the house. One of Wild Apache's common-law wives was entering the living room from the kitchen and screamed when she saw Anthony enter the house armed. He quickly shot her twice in the chest but the screams had alerted the four men that were in the back-yard playing dominoes. They grabbed their high powered weapons and ran to the house. Anthony ran straight to the room beside the back veranda where Wild Apache had said the drugs and money were hidden. Carlos and Juan stood ready with their guns aimed at the sole back entrance to the house. They didn't have to worry about the front entrance; Hernandez had that covered. The first man to enter the house was cut down by a flurry of bullets. The other three cursed and backed up. One decided to approach from the front. He hurried along the side of the house and ran to the front veranda. Hernandez put his window down and blasted a huge hole in his back with the powerful rifle. Anthony found the drugs and money in a large tote bag which he dragged from the room.

The two men were still by the back entrance unsure of what to do. They couldn't enter from the back and the explosion they heard at the front indicated that the front was also covered. One of them took out his cell phone to call for reinforcements. Anthony heaved the heavy bag onto his shoulder and they hurriedly left the house and jumped into the Escalade. Anthony threw the bag in the trunk and got behind the wheel. The tires squealed loudly as Anthony sped off. Three motor bikes came towards them as they drove down the road. Hernandez shot the first rider and the bike skidded into a group of people under the streetlight gambling. Anthony swerved the vehicle and hit one of the other bikes. The rider screamed in agony as his left leg was crushed by the impact. The third rider managed to avoid the SUV and fired several shots at the vehicle. The women screamed as the rear window shattered from the impact of the bullets. No one was hit but the ones closest to the window were covered with shards of broken glass. They made it out to the main road with the motor bike in hot pursuit. Carlos fired a full clip from his semi-automatic assault rifle as Anthony skillfully swerved onto the main road without slowing down. The motorbike toppled as both man and machine received multiple bullet holes.

Anthony breathed a sigh of relief as he turned onto Mountain View Avenue. They had made it. They just needed to hurry and get off the road. The vehicle had been riddled with bullets and would attract a lot of attention. The damaged vehicle received some curious glances from other motorists in traffic. Anthony ignored them and kept his fingers crossed that they would not be stopped by the police. Forty minutes later they turned on the Stony Hill Road and Anthony breathed easier. They unloaded the vehicle when they got home and Juan backed out the Range Rover which was at the front of the spacious garage and Anthony put the Escalade at the front and covered it up. They wouldn't need it again. Hernandez was thoughtful as they went inside the house. He didn't like the way things were turning out. He didn't want to be so close to the action, suppose he had been hit by a bullet just now? He was also disappointed that Wild Apache was taken out of the picture so quickly. Now he would have to regroup and find another underworld connection. Then there was Anthony. Efficient as always but he didn't feel as if he could trust him anymore. He would have to be killed. The ungrateful, insolent pup was getting too big for his britches. He would have Juan and Carlos eliminate him in his sleep. Nothing could go wrong. Anthony was a dangerous man.

Anthony headed for the bathroom immediately. He took a long shower and threw on a hair of sweat pants and went back downstairs. The girls were unusually quiet; shaken into silence by what they had just experienced. They were used to seeing violence but that had been a close call. Anthony switched on the TV and turned to the local station. It was almost time for the eight-thirty news. Maria came downstairs and went into the kitchen for two ice cold coronas. She glanced briefly at Anthony as she climbed the stairs. He watched her as she slowly walked back up the stairs. She had on a T-shirt that barely covered her ass and she did not have on any underwear. Juan frowned as he noticed the interaction between Anthony and Maria. He would tell Hernandez that he suspected that Anthony was fucking Maria. The news came on and the shootout in Rockfort was the lead story. The area was under curfew and the police had cordoned off the entire community. Anthony watched intently as Terri's gorgeous face came into view. She gave a brief interview to the reporter: At approximately seven p.m. shots were heard in the vicinity of the house of reputed area leader Conrad Boorasingh, popularly known as Wild Apache. A black SUV was observed speeding away from the premises and its occupants were engaged in a shootout with three men who were on motorbikes. Those three men were killed. Also found dead at the house where the battle apparently began, were a woman and two men. We are following up on several leads and the area will be under a nine p.m. to nine a.m. curfew for at least the next four days. Thank you.

Anthony got up as they moved on to another story. He went for his cell phone and went out by the poolside to call Terri. Juan took the opportunity to go upstairs and speak to Hernandez. He knocked on the bedroom door.

"Yeah?"

"It's Juan."

"Come in." Hernandez was sitting up in bed with a towel wrapped around his waist. Maria was in the shower.

"I need to talk to you," Juan said to him quietly. They went out to the bedroom balcony. They looked down to see Anthony on a lounge chair by the pool talking on his cell phone. Juan told him his suspicions about Anthony and Maria. Hernandez eyes narrowed. He told Juan to quickly fetch Carlos. When they came back he told them that Anthony was to be executed in his sleep later this week. He needed him for a few more days then he would give the order. He would deal with Maria on his own. She would learn in painful fashion what happened to double crossing putas. Maria tiptoed back into the bathroom unseen. She had heard the knock on the door and noticed when Hernandez and Juan had gone on the balcony. She had left the shower running and hid behind the folded balcony doors and listened to their conversation. She trembled as she stood under the shower. Juan was such a pussy! What he told Hernandez wasn't even true. At least not yet. She shuddered when she thought of what Hernandez might do to her. She had to warn Anthony. She turned the shower off and got out. She dried herself and went into the bedroom. Hernandez was reclined in the bed smoking a cigar wearing a stoic expression.

"Come here bitch," He commanded.

Maria tried not to show any fear and went to him on the bed. He threw off his towel and exposed his erection. She started to fellate him. Maria winced as Hernandez groaned and gripped her long hair painfully. She ignored the pain and applied herself to the task at hand. Hernandez had once confided to her that she gave him the best sex he had ever had. She hoped her skills would spare her life long enough for Anthony to kill Hernandez before he harmed her.

Anthony took a dip in the pool after he had finished talking to Terri. He had gotten her while she was on her way to police head-quarters. She had seemed a bit reserved but he attributed that to her probably being tired as well as being around her co-workers. He swam two more laps and then went inside. Everyone except Hernandez and Maria were in the living room hanging out. He went into the kitchen and grabbed a beer. He paused at the doorway and looked briefly at the pornography the others were watching on the TV. There were two guys and a busty blonde going at it in the woods. Anthony then went upstairs to take a shower. He was in the shower for five minutes when he heard the bathroom door open and shut quickly. He shoved aside the shower curtain. It was Maria.

"Where's Hernandez?" Anthony asked, surprised at her boldness.

"He's sleeping. He'll be out for at least four hours." She smiled wickedly. "I just gave him my special."

Anthony didn't respond. Maria shrugged off her robe and stepped into the shower, closing the shower curtain behind her. She faced Anthony and stood inches away from him as the water cascaded down her back.

"Hernandez is going to kill you, this week," Maria told him, looking directly in his intense grey eyes.

"How would you know that?" Anthony responded as he took the soap and began to lather her body.

"Juan sneaked upstairs to the room earlier and told him that you are fucking me". She closed her eyes and her lips quivered as Anthony rubbed the soap sensuously on her breasts. She continued, "I sneaked out of the shower and eavesdropped while they were talking on the balcony."

She braced one hand on the shower wall for support as Anthony rubbed the soap lightly over her pubic area. Her legs trembled when his hand rubbed her now protruding clitoris.

"Tell me more." He put the soap down and turned her around, stepping up closely to her from behind. She could feel his erection poking her in the lower back.

"He...said...that he needed...you for...a...ohhhh," Maria moaned as Anthony inserted two fingers inside her while rubbing her clit insistently with his thumb. "He needs you for a couple more days...hmm....ohh...yes...and then...he will order Juan and his brother to kill you in your sleep..." Maria started to grind against Anthony as her orgasm approached.

"What about you?" Anthony asked, not sure if he believed her story.

"He's...going ..to...kill...me...too...*dios mio*!" she exclaimed as she climaxed.

Anthony shoved his dick inside her while she came. She gasped and felt the spasms intensify as he started to move slowly inside her. She placed her hands on the shower wall and bent over a bit, thrusting her ass up against him as she came again and again. Anthony increased his pace as he felt her juices bathe him over and over. No wonder Hernandez was pussy-whipped Anthony mused. Maria's pussy was no joke. She lifted her right leg and Anthony held on to it as he drove in and out of her with deep, hard strokes.

"You better not be lying to me Maria," he said as he felt his orgasm building up. "I won't hesitate to mess up your pretty face if I find out you're bullshitting me."

"Nooo...I'm...telling...you...the... truth," Maria breathed as she felt yet another orgasm threatening to wrack her body. This had to be a record.

Anthony grunted as he shot a torrid load of semen inside Maria. Her knees wobbled and Anthony had to hold her up as she came for the sixth time in ten minutes.

They were silent for a few minutes as they stood under the water flowing from the shower head. Maria then reached for the soap and cleaned both of them.

"I'm gonna take care of everything," Anthony promised as Maria dried herself off and put on her robe.

"I know you will," she responded and cautiously opened the bathroom the door. Then she was gone. Anthony sat on the toilet seat and digested what Maria had told him. Juan was an ungrateful bastard, he mused. I was the one that bought him and his brother to the organization and look how easy it was for him to carry my name to Hernandez. Anthony knew that when he had challenged Hernandez downstairs that he would eventually try to kill him so he wasn't surprised that Hernandez wouldn't have asked him about it before deciding to harm him. It was all a moot point anyway. Hernandez's death warrant had long been signed when Maria had told him what Hernandez had done to his mother. Anthony got up and went to his room feeling invigorated. He was in his element. Killing all three of them would be almost as enjoyable as the sex he just had with Maria. Almost.

CHAPTER 9

Terri was exhausted when she got home at ten that night. It had been a very hectic day. She quickly peeled off her clothes and ran a bubble bath. She went into the kitchen for a glass of white wine, put on her Beres Hammond CD, lit her scented candles and settled in the bath. It felt heavenly. She sipped her wine and sang along with Beres as she tried not to think about work or Anthony. Forty-five minutes later, she felt much better and got out of the bathroom. She rummaged through her T-shirt draw and put on a baby T that read *Don't feed the models*. Anna had given it to her. She then slipped on a tight fitting sweat pants and went into the kitchen to get something to eat. She made herself a turkey and cheese sandwich, grabbed a bottle of Gatorade and curled up in front of the TV. She felt for something silly so she settled on HBO which was showing a comedy. She ate and laughed at Eddie Griffin's antics. Her cell phone rang from where she had left it on the coffee-table. Terri groaned and reached for it, hoping it wasn't a police emergency. It was Anthony.

"Hi Tony," she said.

"Hey baby. Everything ok?"

"Yeah, today was a really long day. I'm soooo tired."

"I was hoping to see you tonight but it's ok...you turn in early and get some rest," Anthony said.

"Ok Tony. I'll call you tomorrow," Terri replied.

"Yeah, bye." Anthony ended the call. He was lying on his bed, naked. He had been like this since he got out of the shower hours ago. His door was closed but not locked and the light was off. He was totally relaxed and his guns were in easy reach — just in case Hernandez changed his mind and decided to strike early. Anthony yawned. Not from sleep but from hunger. He hadn't eaten since he had lunch on the yacht. He felt like going into New Kingston to get something to eat. He switched on the light and went to the closet. He selected a pair of Just Cavalli jeans and threw on the matching jacket over a white T-shirt. He put on his dark blue Timberland boots, grabbed one of his guns and went out the door. Hernandez was downstairs eating pizza when he went down to the living room. Juan was watching him with a smirk. Anthony ignored him.

"Hey padre," Anthony said as he grabbed the keys to the Range Rover from the hook near the TV. "I'm going out for a bit."

"Ok, Tony," Hernandez replied through a mouthful of ground beef and cheese.

Anthony drove out and headed down Stony Hill Road. He opened the moon roof and lowered the windows. There was a nice, cool breeze blowing. He turned on the radio and settled on Irie FM. Latino music was his first love but he loved reggae too; especially the older stuff. He thought about his life as he turned onto Constant Spring Road. Things were about to change drastically. Once he killed Hernandez he would have access to at least six million US dollars in hard cash. There was money in the safe at the villa back in Cuba and there was money in the safe in the master bedroom at the Jamaican mansion. There was also legitimate money in various accounts that Gavin the lawyer had opened on their behalf. He could instruct Gavin to withdraw the funds and close those accounts. Prime real estate. Luxurious cars. He would be a very wealthy man. He could leave the drug game alone if he wanted to. A rich, retired drug dealer at twenty-seven. Not bad for a little kid who grew up on the mean streets of Havana not knowing where his next meal was coming from. But what would he retire and do? He loved the excitement and danger of being in the drug game. He loved to kill people. Well, I'll cross that bridge when I get there Anthony mused as he waited for the stoplight to turn green. First things first, Hernandez, Juan and Carlos, and that crusty cop Mayweather all had to die over the next couple of days.

"Wonder where that son of a bitch is off to?" Hernandez remarked. He was reclined on the lounge chair out by the poolside drinking champagne with Juan and Carlos. The women were inside and Maria was upstairs in his bedroom. "After he's gone, you boys will be my eyes and ears. I'm going to have to send for some more soldiers to come out here to Jamaica. Juan, you will go to Cuba and handpick eight men to help handle things out here."

"Si, padre." Juan grinned and sipped his champagne. Things were looking up already and that bastard Anthony wasn't even dead yet. He couldn't wait to slit his throat, as soon as Hernandez gave the word.

"I'll send for the Cessna on Friday to pick you up," Hernandez continued. "You should be back by Sunday." He picked up his cell phone and called his lawyer.

"Gavin, did everything go smoothly with the transaction today?" Hernandez asked when Gavin came on the line.

"Hey Pablo, yeah, everything is on stream," he replied. "By the end of the week transfer of ownership will be complete."

"Good," Hernandez responded. "I want to go down to Negril soon. The property is really nice. Reminds me of my villa in Cuba."

"Well, that should be possible by next weekend," Gavin told him. "You're getting the place completely furnished."

"Ok. What's happening with that merchant banker that you're supposed to hook me up with?"

"He was off the island on vacation and just returned today. I'll set up a meeting by Thursday."

"Alright, seems like you're on top of everything. We'll talk." Hernandez hung up the phone and gestured for Juan to refill his glass.

"So you boys want to have some fun with Maria?" Hernandez asked the brothers with a cruel smile.

Juan and Carlos grinned. "Hell yeah!" they both gushed at the same time.

"Ok, let's go upstairs and have some fun with that double crossing puta." They rose and went upstairs.

Anthony reached New Kingston and parked in the private parking lot opposite the Asylum Night Club on the hip strip. He paid his fee and tipped the attendant twenty US dollars. The man grinned and thanked him heartily. On a whim, he asked the man if he knew where he could get some pure heroin to buy; just a small quantity. The man was suspicious at first but Anthony calmed his fears by showing him his gun. The man visibly relaxed. He knew that the police did not carry Berattas so he knew Anthony was a gangster. The man told Anthony that anything could be had in New Kingston if one knew who to ask. He told Anthony to go ahead and go to his destination, when he returned for his vehicle he would have the heroin waiting for him. Anthony thanked him and strolled across the street, making his way to the restaurant next to the club. The strip was fairly busy for a Monday night. There was a long queue at the entrance of the club. The women were dressed in the latest dancehall fashions and chattered noisily as they waited to get into the club. Anthony went into the restaurant and sat alone at a corner table. He ordered barbeque wings and garlic bread. He looked around as he waited for his order. A group of four young women were seated at a table close to him having burgers. They were obviously going clubbing after their meal. The one with the blonde weave eyed Anthony flirtatiously and whispered something to the other girls who laughed at her comment. Anthony ignored them. Two men were seated at a corner table sharing a large plate of French fries. After watching for a couple seconds Anthony realized it was a gay couple. He was surprised as he had heard stories of homosexuals being beaten and even killed if discovered in public. Jamaica was renowned for being a homophobic society. Guess times are changing Anthony thought as his order arrived.

Maria's pretty face wore a look of terror when the trio of Hernandez, Juan and Carlos entered the bedroom. Her hands were handcuffed to the headboard and she was nude. She had been in this position a lot of times when role-playing with Hernandez but this was no game. Earlier when she had gotten back to the room after being in the shower with Anthony, Hernandez had been sleeping so she had put some clothes on and went to relax by the pool. Hernandez had woken up earlier than usual and pissed that she was not in the room when he got up, he hollered for her to get her ass upstairs. When she came up he had slapped her around and told her to take off her clothes. He then cuffed her to the bed. Now he was back with the brothers and Maria knew what was coming next. Tears began to stream down her face.

"Aww, the whore is crying...how sweet," Hernandez mocked as the brothers removed her from the bed and took her out onto the balcony. "You should have thought about the consequences before you decided to double cross me bitch."

"I didn't....." Maria protested tearfully as Hernandez slapped her hard across the face.

"Shut up!" Hernandez said.

Juan and Carlos cuffed her to the rails on the balcony. Her back was to her tormentors and the lovely view of Kingston city was facing her. Hernandez grabbed a chair and sat down. He lit a cigar and gestured for the show to begin. Juan and Carlos grinned maliciously and stripped off their clothes. Hernandez watched with a satisfied smirk as Juan and Carlos took turns raping Maria. She screamed as they penetrated and sodomized her mercilessly. The other women were downstairs chilling and heard her screams. They were unsympathetic. The general consensus was that Maria had made her bed and now she had to lie in it.

Anthony finished his meal and exited the restaurant. As promised, the man had the heroin. Anthony paid him and gave him another big tip. The man told Anthony that anything he needed, anytime, just let him know. Anthony took his cell number, hopped into the Range Rover and made his way back to Stony Hill. The traffic was light and he got home in forty minutes. Everyone except Maria was downstairs watching an old gangster movie when he stepped inside. He grunted a greeting and went upstairs. Nobody really answered. He smiled to himself as he climbed the stairs. Even the women had chosen sides. Oh well, he would dispose of them as well. He locked his door and stripped down to his boxers and went to bed with his gun within easy reach on the bedside table.

The next morning, Hernandez received a call from his associate in Miami. They needed some product urgently as they lost some kilos in an unexpected raid by the police. Hernandez advised him that he had thirty-six kilos handy that he could have packaged and be ready for delivery later that day. The man promised to call Hernandez back by midday. He would send a small plane to meet the yacht at a point to be determined to collect the cocaine. Hernandez got up out of bed and went to take a shower. Ten minutes later he came out of the bathroom and stood looking at Maria. Last night after they had finished assaulting her, Juan and Carlos had uncuffed her and Maria had limped slowly and painfully to the bathroom to get cleaned up. When she was through, Hernandez instructed them to cuff one of her hands to the bed foot. That was where she had slept. She looked at him, her sultry eyes blazing with hatred. She was in excruciating pain and needed medical attention.

"Aren't you sorry you double crossed me?" He asked as he went over to the closet to select something to wear.

Maria did not reply. Hernandez got dressed and called for Juan and Carlos. He told them to get ready as they would be leaving out early to get some breakfast and go out to the yacht.

"What about her?" Juan asked.

"She'll stay right where she is until we get back," Hernandez responded coldly. "On second thought, release her and lock the balcony and bedroom door. I want her to have access to the bathroom. She might have a problem with her bowels and I don't want shit all over my carpet." The brothers laughed and left the room to wake up the women and get ready. Anthony heard the activity in the house and got up out of bed. He did ten sets of push ups to loosen his muscles and went to take a shower. Hernandez was waiting in his room went he got back.

"We need to go out to the yacht," Hernandez told him.

"Ok," he responded. "What's up?"

Hernandez filled him in on the phone call he had received from Miami and then left him to get dressed. Everyone was ready to go in twenty minutes.

"Where's Maria?" Anthony asked as they piled into the Range Rover.

"She's staying home today," Hernandez responded. "She's not feeling too well."

Juan snickered from the back. Anthony drove out without further comment. They stopped at a restaurant on the way out of Kingston and got some breakfast. Anthony wondered what the hell they had done to Maria while he ate. He decided then and there that he would kill them all tonight. Fuck all this waiting and unnecessary tension.

Terri arrived at headquarters at 8:30 feeling energized. She had gotten a restful sleep last night. Her head was clear and she was in a buoyant mood. She checked her messages when she got to her office. Shit, the Commissioner had called to inform her that he wasn't coming in until Thursday. She was looking forward to see him today. The immigration officer had also called. She had called him yesterday to see if there was any information on Pablo Hernandez and Anthony Garcia. She picked up the phone and dialed his direct line.

"Hello."

"Mr. Foster, good morning, it's Detective Miller," Terri said pleasantly.

"Morning, Detective, I checked on the names you requested and there is nothing on them in our database. No record of Pablo Hernandez and Anthony Garcia ever entering the country."

Terri was silent for a moment. "Thanks for your help, Mr. Foster."

"Anytime, Detective."

Shit, Terri thought as she hung up the phone. They needed to have a serious talk. She decided to invite him for lunch, start picking his brain. She could no longer ignore the fact that Anthony was obviously mixed up in illegal activities.

Mayweather met with his special unit at his home a few minutes before nine that morning. He told them that the plan to execute Hernandez and his cohorts was definitely on. They were to standby at seven that evening for his call. Once he confirmed that the targets were at home, they would meet at the gas station at the bottom of Stony Hill and proceed to the mansion. The meeting ended and the men left. Mayweather then hopped in his truck and headed to the office. He smiled as he turned on the radio. Today would be a good day.

Hernandez dialed Gavin's number as they left the restaurant and headed out to Port Royal.

"Gavin I need you to get me a new SUV," He said.

"Ok... you're tired of the ones you have already?" Gavin asked, surprised. All three vehicles Hernandez had in Jamaica were pretty much new.

"Yeah, something like that," Hernandez replied. "I want a black Hummer, place the order today."

"Will do," Gavin responded.

Hernandez ended the call and reclined in his seat. They got to the harbour twenty minutes later. Anthony parked and everyone alighted from the vehicle and went onboard the yacht, with Juan and Carlos carrying the tote bag with the cocaine. The two crew members who were responsible for packaging the product took the drugs below deck to package it together with the twenty kilos that they already had. Hernandez instructed the chef to start preparing some lunch and gestured for one of the women to give him a massage. Anthony changed into beach shorts and relaxed in a shaded area on deck. His gun was tucked in his waist and he sipped cold lemonade to battle the heat. Juan came back upstairs and shot Anthony a smirk as he walked by. Anthony was bit annoyed at the manner in which Juan had been looking at him since yesterday. He decided to embarrass him. Anthony got up and casually walked over to where Juan had sat down between two of the women. He smiled coldly at Juan and swiftly gave him a hard punch in his right eye. The women screamed and got out of the way as Anthony followed up the punch with two back-handed slaps.

"Tony!" Hernandez shouted, "What the fuck are you doing?!"

Anthony ignored him and whipped out his gun, training it on Carlos who had come running with his gun drawn when he heard the commotion. "This little punk keeps looking at me disrespectfully. He needed a lesson."

"It's not your place to discipline him Tony!" Hernandez was livid. "You come to me if you've got a problem with one of my soldiers!"

"Well now you know padre," Anthony snarled derisively.

"Lower your weapon Carlos!" Hernandez instructed. He walked over to look at Juan's face. The area around his right eye was puffy and discoloured. It was swelling rapidly and he could hardly see out of it. "Fuck!" Hernandez cursed. "He needs to see a doctor."

Anthony looked at him coldly and tucked his gun back in his waist. "Oh he'll be fine. He's a tough guy, right?" Anthony chuckled and went back to the shaded area to sit down. Carlos went over to his brother and whispered something in his ear. Hernandez told one of the women to accompany the brothers downstairs and use one the first aid kits to dress Juan's eye until they went back into Kingston. Hernandez shook his head and cursed to himself. Anthony was out of control. He deeply regretted deciding to wait before having him killed. That shall be rectified tonight. Anthony will not live to see tomorrow.

Anthony's cell phone rang a few minutes later. It was Terri.

"Hi babe," Anthony drawled.

"My, my, don't we sound relaxed," Terri remarked. "Are you free for lunch?"

"Sorry baby; can't make it," Anthony replied. "I have some business I have to take care off."

"That's too bad Mr. Businessman. I was looking forward to gazing in your sexy eyes while I ate."

Anthony chuckled. "I'll try and make it up to you tonight."

"I'm holding you to that...don't make me have to arrest you," Terri joked.

Anthony laughed. "I'll talk to you later, sugar."

"Make sure, we need to talk. Bye, Tony."

Anthony poured himself some more lemonade and lit a cigar. He wondered what Terri wanted to talk to him about. He checked the time. It was now 11:30. He hoped the guy from Miami called soon as he didn't want to be out here all day. Carlos came back upstairs and went over to Hernandez. He told him Juan's eye was bandaged and he was resting as it was paining him badly. Hernandez nodded and told him to tell the chef to hurry up with lunch. He was getting hungry. He wondered if Juan would be in any shape to assist in murdering Anthony tonight. If not, he would have to help Carlos; one man could not get the job done. Anthony was a killing machine.

Terri had lunch with her second option; her mother. They met at the Rib Shack and had barbequed spare ribs.

"How is Anna?" Mrs. Miller asked, as she dabbed the corners of her mouth daintily.

"She's good," Terri replied. "I had lunch with her yesterday."

"I haven't seen her in ages. Is she still modeling?"

"Yeah, but she mostly does catalogue stuff and magazines these days." Terri ate the last of her spare ribs and leaned back contentedly in her chair.

"How is your love life? I notice you have a little glow," her mom said, fishing.

Terri laughed. "I'm glowing?"

"Yep. Either you're pregnant or you've met somebody," she replied, adding, "I hope it's the latter."

"Of course I'm not pregnant Mom!" Terri exclaimed. "I haven't met anyone either."

"Hmmm…" her mother said unconvinced. "Whatever you say dear."

"When I meet someone you'll be the first to know Mum," Terri said. She had no intention of telling her mom about Anthony. Not yet anyway. There were some questions that needed answering.

"Your father won't leave me alone since he started taking Levitra," her mother remarked, changing the subject. "He's been chasing me around the house like he's sixteen years old."

"Mom! That's way too much information," Terri said laughing. They chatted for a few more minutes and then left the crowded restaurant. Terri went back to the office and her mom went to the gym for aerobics class.

Hernandez's associate from Miami finally called at 12:30. He told him a small aircraft would meet them forty miles outside of Port Royal at approximately 1:45 to make the pick up. Hernandez hung up the phone and instructed the crew to sail out to the designated co-ordinates. The chef carried lunch on deck and everyone dug in hungrily. He had prepared crab cakes, buffalo wings, pumpkin rice and fried potatoes. One of the girls took a plate down to Juan to se if he could manage to eat. The entire right side of his face was badly swollen.

They turned off the boat engine and waited for signs of the plane. It was now ten minutes to two. At two o' clock they saw the plane flying very low and it circled them twice before landing and stopping thirty feet from the yacht. Hernandez waved a greeting to the pilot and two of the crew members dressed in diving gear jumped overboard and took the two packages to the plane. They quickly loaded the plane, which used the clear blue sea as its runway and took off noisily. Hernandez, satisfied, lit a cigar and called Miami to let them know that the drugs had been successfully picked up.

Maria felt weak and tired as she lay on the bathroom floor. Since Hernandez left she had been to the bathroom so many times she decided to just stay there. It was too painful to be moving back and forth. She was also famished. Her last meal had been early in the afternoon yesterday. Anthony was her only hope of survival. Maria leaned her head against the side of the bath and prayed.

CHAPTER 10

The yacht got back to Port Royal at 3 p.m. Hernandez fumed but remained silent when he realized Anthony was taking his own sweet time to come to the vehicle. Everyone stood around the Range Rover waiting on Anthony as he casually made his way from below deck where he had gone to change his clothes. He opened the truck and everyone got in. Hernandez called Gavin as Anthony turned onto the main road leading back into Kingston.

"Gavin, where is the closest hospital? I'm on my way into town from Port Royal," he said.

"Go to St. Michael's, its on Deanary Road off Mountain View Avenue." Gavin told him. "What's wrong?"

"Juan had an accident," Hernandez said and ended the call.

He gave Anthony the directions to the hospital and they got there in thirty minutes. Anthony stayed outside smoking a cigar as everyone else went inside. They finally emerged from the hospital an hour later. Juan was now sporting a fresh bandage which completely covered the injured eye. Hernandez sent Carlos to fill the prescriptions at the pharmacy which was on the premises. He came back in ten minutes with the medication for his brother and Anthony drove out.

Hernandez was furious. The eye had been badly damaged. An X-ray had revealed that a bone close to the eye had been bent out of position and Juan would require surgery if he was to ever see properly again. The doctor had given him the number for a specialist that would be able to perform the operation. Hernandez would call him tomorrow to see how quickly they could schedule the operation. This means he would have to go to Cuba himself to select a new team to hold the fort down in Jamaica. Carlos was willing but he wasn't the sharpest knife in the drawer. Hernandez couldn't entrust him with that kind of responsibility.

Assistant Commissioner Mayweather was at his desk looking for his private phonebook. He needed to make an important overseas call. He called home, thinking maybe he had left it there. The phone rang without an answer. Fuck! He fumed, where the hell is that woman? He dialed his wife's cell phone. She answered after the third ring.

"Hello," Elaine Mayweather said as she pushed the trolley down the hygiene products aisle.

"Where the hell are you? You didn't tell me you were leaving the house," Mayweather demanded harshly.

But what is wrong with this man dear lord, Elaine thought, thoroughly annoyed. Aloud she said, "Claude, I didn't know I needed your permission to leave the house but if you must know I'm at the supermarket."

Mayweather bristled at her reply. "Yuh eat too fucking much, every damn day yuh gone ah supermarket. No wonder yuh so big and sour."

Elaine was stung by his cruel comments but did not respond. She wondered if her husband was on drugs.

"Hurry up and go home. When you get there find my little black phonebook and call me. There's a number in there that I need urgently." He hung up without waiting for a response.

Elaine had had enough of her husband's bullshit. She decided after leaving the supermarket she would go by the cinema to watch the afternoon matinee. If he needs the number so badly let him go home and get it himself. She smiled and turned off her cell phone. She hummed as she picked up a couple bars of her favourite soap. It felt good to stand up to the bastard.

An hour passed and Mayweather realized his wife hadn't called him back yet. He dialed her cell number. It went straight to voicemail. He dialed the house number. It rang without an answer. He grabbed his car keys angrily. She would pay dearly tonight for making him having to leave the office and go back home to look for his phonebook.

Anthony pulled up at the mansion at 4 p.m. He hurriedly went inside as he wanted to be the first one upstairs. He figured Maria had to be in Hernandez's bedroom and he wanted to know if she was ok. He walked quickly to the front door while the others were still getting out of the vehicle. When he entered the house and none of them could see him, he sprinted up the stairs.

He stood by Hernandez's bedroom door.

"Maria," he said. No answer.

"Maria!" he said, a little louder this time.

"Tony?" Her voice sounded weak.

"Are you ok?" He could hear the others downstairs. Someone turned on the TV.

She said something but he couldn't hear her. She was obviously in pain. "Sit tight. I'm gonna get you out," Anthony said and quickly moved away from the door and went into the bathroom. Carlos was helping his brother up the stairs and Hernandez was right behind them. He left the bathroom door open and started to piss. Juan and Carlos went into their room and Anthony heard when Hernandez put his key into the door. As soon as he opened the door Anthony quickly stepped up behind him.

"Padre...." Anthony began, pretending to ask him a question.

Hernandez, startled, could not stop Anthony from entering the room without giving him a hard push and he didn't think that would be a good idea.

Anthony looked at Maria's nude body on the floor. She was barely conscious.

Hernandez looked grim. "I have things to attend to Tony. Excuse me for awhile."

"Sure, but I'm taking her out of here. She obviously needs medical attention," Anthony replied in a tone that implied he would not be deterred.

"This dosen't concern you Anthony!" Hernandez snarled. "She's my property."

Anthony ignored him and lifted Maria from off the floor. He whipped out his gun as Carlos barged into the room armed.

"Ok, ok...everybody be cool," Hernandez said. He was furious but he decided to exercise a little patience. Anthony would get what's coming to him soon enough. He instructed Carlos to put away his weapon. Anthony kept his gun drawn but lowered it. Anthony ordered Carlos to go in the closet and grab a top and jeans for Maria. He cursed under his breath but did as he was told. Anthony gestured for him to place them over his shoulder and then took Maria to his room. He heard the door slam behind him.

"I knew you'd save me…" Maria said softly, grimacing in pain as Anthony dressed her.

"Sshh," Anthony responded. "Save your strength." He finished putting on her clothes and carried her outside the bedroom. He locked the door behind him. He knew that they were going to try and ambush him when he got back to the house and he wanted to limit their options.

The rest of the women were downstairs and they watched silently as Anthony, with Maria thrown over his shoulder, grabbed the keys to the BMW and left the house.

He gently settled Maria in the front seat and put on her seat belt. He then hopped in and headed out. He whipped out his cell phone and called the man who had supplied him with the heroin. He asked him which hospital was the best in Kingston and got directions. Anthony arrived at Caribbean University Hospital fifty minutes later and took Maria to the emergency ward. After speaking at length to the doctor, he filled out some paperwork and gave them two thousand US dollars as a deposit for her stay, pending the final bill. He told the doctor that money was no object. Whatever he needed to do he should just carry on and give him a call on his cell phone to update him on her condition.

Anthony checked the time as he drove off the hospital compound. It was 6:05. He decided to stop at a sports bar in New Kingston and have a drink before heading back to the house. At the stoplight he checked the two guns he had with him to make sure the clips were full. He was going to kill everyone when he got back to the house. Anthony stopped at the sports bar and purchased a chilled bottle of Hypnotic. He hopped back in the car which he had double-parked in front of the bar and headed home. He sipped from the bottle. At the stoplight on Hope Road, a matronly woman in the adjacent lane, driving an old Mercedes looked at him disapprovingly and said something. He put his window down and looked at her questioningly.

"You shouldn't drink and drive, young man," she said sharply.

"I'm drinking while I drive," Anthony replied, grinning. "There's a difference."

The woman shook her head and Anthony sped off as the light changed to green. Anthony got home at 6:55 and parked the car in the garage. He hopped out of the car, carrying the now half-empty bottle of Hypnotic in his hand. Hernandez's cell phone rang as he entered the house. Everyone was downstairs except for Juan. He went into the kitchen and placed the bottle in the refrigerator. Hernandez got off his cell phone and gestured for one of the girls to pour him some more champagne. He did not look at Anthony.

Anthony smiled to himself and went upstairs. He planned to take a nice shower, pack his clothes, kill everyone and get a penthouse suite at the luxurious Regal Court Hotel in New Kingston. He would stay there until he decided his next move. He locked the bathroom door and placed his guns within easy reach. He hummed his favourite Carlos Santana song as he showered.

Mayweather was seated in his SUV at the gas station at the foot of Stony Hill Road. He had just called his special unit to let them know that all the targets were home and he was waiting for them at the agreed meeting point. He had called Hernandez under the pretext of checking in to see if all was well with his operations. Casually he had asked him if Anthony was there. Hernandez had snorted a terse 'yeah'. Mayweather wondered what that was about. Seems like there's trouble in the camp. He saw a black jeep turn into the gas station. The team had arrived. The four men alighted from the jeep and came to sit in Mayweather's truck.

"Ok, here's the plan gentlemen," Mayweather said. "The only exits are the kitchen door and the front door. So once you go in, anyone upstairs will be cornered. Unless they try to climb down the balcony which is dangerous as it's fairly high." He cleared his throat and continued. "So you enter swiftly through the front door, its usually unlocked, and shoot everyone in sight. Then you head upstairs and go through every room. Absolutely no survivors, gentlemen. When the mission is completed, switch the living room light on and off three times. That's the signal that the coast is clear. I'll then enter the house and we'll divide up the spoils. Let's go."

The men went back into the jeep and both vehicles pulled out, Mayweather in front. They got to the mansion in twenty minutes and Mayweather turned off his lights and parked on the lawn close to the entrance to the property. The other men turned the light off on the jeep and drove it slowly towards the house. They stopped about a hundred and fifty feet from the garage and parked the jeep.

"Let's do this," Sgt. Brown said and all four men alighted from the vehicle with their guns ready. They crouched and made their way to the house. At this time, Hernandez gestured to Carlos and they went up to his room. Hernandez lit a cigar and he started to discuss with Carlos the best way to annihilate Anthony.

Anthony was in his room packing when he heard the barrage of gun shots downstairs. He quickly grabbed his two Berretas and cautiously opened his bedroom door. Carlos stepped out of Hernandez's room with his gun drawn as well, Hernandez in tow, looking alarmed. Anthony whispered that they were obviously under attack and told Hernandez to get back into his room. He told Carlos to follow him. They ventured closely to the top of the stairs and crouched, waiting.

After entering the house and killing the five women that were downstairs watching TV, they realized that the men must be upstairs. They crouched and tried to cover each other as they proceeded to climb the winding staircase. Anthony killed the first one to climb the stairs with a clean shot to the neck. He toppled over and they retreated quickly.

"Bloodclaat, Mackie dead," Sgt. Brown said, stating the obvious. They needed to get upstairs another way. Sgt. Brown instructed the other two to retrieve the rope from the truck and one should scale the balcony while the other covered him from the ground. He would stay in here and prevent anyone from coming down the stairs. They rushed off to do his bidding.

Anthony told Carlos to stand guard at the top of the stairs and he went into Hernandez's bedroom. Hernandez was holding a pump rifle and he was standing by the door.

"Listen, I'm going to climb down the balcony and go downstairs, cover me." Anthony knew Hernandez wouldn't shoot him in the back as they both knew he was their only chance of surviving this unexpected attack. Hernandez nodded and Anthony went on the balcony. He looked down and figured he could jump from there onto the large lounge chair that was under the balcony at the poolside. He crouched on the top of the rails and jumped down with both guns in his hands. He landed on the chair, and bounced off expertly, breaking his fall by rolling over. The two policemen came around the corner as Anthony straightened up from the ground. They all saw each other at the same time but Anthony was quicker to react. He fired the two guns simultaneously, accurately hitting the men in the face and neck. He avoided the torso knowing they would be wearing bulletproof vests. He was grazed on his left arm by a bullet from one of the men, but was otherwise unharmed. Anthony then cautiously made his way around the corner to the front of the house.

Sgt. Brown could smell his own body odour as he began to sweat profusely. Things were definitely not going as planned. He had heard the shots outside and somehow felt that his men had gotten the wrong end of the stick. He decided to retreat. He turned and went through the front door. Anthony crouched by the wall and was about to make his move when he saw a man hurry out the front door. Anthony wanted him alive. He fired three shots and the man squealed and toppled over firing his weapon as he fell. Anthony leaned back against the wall until he heard click click. The man's clip was empty. Anthony moved quickly and trained his gun on the injured man who was moaning in pain and trying to insert a fresh clip in his weapon.

"Drop the gun!" Anthony ordered as he approached the man. He did as he was told.

"Mi ah police, nuh kill me," the man said.

When he said that Anthony thought one word; Mayweather. "Is that right," Anthony replied, "Who sent you?"

The man did not respond and Anthony shot him in the arm; twice. The man yelped and grabbed his arm. Anthony stood over him and placed the gun on his chin.

"Mayweather," the man gasped.

"I figured," Anthony said, "Where is that coward?"

"H...him...p...park out ah de gate," the man stammered.

Anthony blew his brains out and started walking out to the gate. He whipped out his cell phone and dialed Mayweather's number.

Mayweather's cell phone rang startling him. He was antsy as he hadn't expected things to take this long. He had heard the exchange of gunfire and figured he should have received the ok signal by now. He looked at the caller ID. Shit. Garcia. That could only mean one thing. Mayweather gunned his engine and quickly drove off the premises. Anthony grinned when he saw the vehicle drive off. He could catch him in the BMW but he'd catch up with Mayweather some other time. He turned and walked back to the house.

Carlos and Hernandez conferred at the top of the stairs. They checked in on Juan who was still fast asleep in his bed. He was heavily medicated and dead to the world. They weren't sure what had transpired since Anthony went downstairs. They decided to cautiously head downstairs and find out what's happening. Hernandez instructed Carlos to shoot Anthony on sight if he was still alive. With Carlos leading the way, they slowly went down the stairs.

Anthony ran up by where he had left the two dead bodies close to the pool side. He picked up the coil of rope that was lying beside one of the men and expertly threw it at the balcony rail. The hook caught in the rail and he quickly climbed up the wall. Carlos and Hernandez reached the bottom of the stairs and were greeted by the bodies of the five dead women. Even the TV had been shot.

Anthony entered the bedroom quietly. He didn't hear anything upstairs so he figured that they had made their way down. He exited Hernandez's bedroom and went into Juan's room. He was sleeping. Anthony removed his sharp pocket knife and stabbed Juan in the good eye. Anthony covered his mouth to stifle his screams and then slit his throat. He then left the bedroom and headed downstairs.

Hernandez and Carlos cautiously went through the front door. They looked grimly at the dead man's brain scattered all over the porch. Hernandez gestured for Carlos to go around the corner to the poolside. He gripped the shot gun tightly and stayed a couple paces behind Carlos.

Anthony reached downstairs and carefully approached the kitchen to make sure no one was hiding behind the kitchen counter. He then made his way outside. Hernandez and Carlos tensed when they saw the bodies of the two men. They realized that Anthony was very much alive. Deep down Hernandez had known he would be; he was just hoping to get lucky. What now?

"Let's get the fuck out of here," Hernandez said to Carlos. "We'll get the keys and just drive out to the yacht. We'll regroup from there."

"But what about Juan?" Carlos asked.

"Juan might be dead Carlos!" Hernandez replied, "I'm not…"

"He is," Anthony said coming around the corner with his gun trained on both of them. "Drop 'em. Now."

Carlos hesitated and Anthony fired a single shot to the middle of his forehead. He died instantly.

Hernandez gasped but still held on to the shot gun.

"Drop it padre," Anthony instructed.

Hernandez stared at him for a long moment and put the gun down. Anthony kept his gun on him and removed the handcuffs from the belt of one of the dead cops. He then walked up to Hernandez and told him to hold his hands out. He snapped the cuffs on and told him to go inside the house.

"Twelve years, Tony," Hernandez said as they went inside the house. "I took you in twelve years ago. And this is how you repay me?"

Anthony directed him up the stairs and didn't respond.

"I treated you like a son! I took you off the streets and made you into something! I created you!"

Anthony remained silent.

"But it wasn't enough for you that you were living a life of luxury, you wanted to be the boss…you're an ungrateful fucker Anthony!"

Anthony listened to him rant until they reached Hernandez's bedroom. Anthony pushed him in and made him sit on a chair. He then removed the cuffs and instructed Hernandez to put his hands behind him, and cuffed him to the chair. He then got two neck ties out of the closet and tied Hernandez's legs to the chair.

"I'll be right back," Anthony said to him pleasantly. He went into his room and retrieved the heroin and drug paraphernalia that he had purchased.

"That's what you think this is about, huh, you piece of shit?" Anthony said to him when he returned. "I don't give a fuck about being the boss. I decided to kill you when I found out what you did to my mother."

Hernandez's eyes widened in surprise.

" Yeah, Maria told me," Anthony informed him. "You deserve to be tortured before I kill you but there's no time. That faggot Mayweather might try to get smart and send the police up here. So, I'll just get right to it."

"Tony...don't do this man...we can bounce back from this," Hernandez begged as Anthony prepared the heroin and filled the needle. "It can be just like old times Tony...we forgive...and forget."

"See you in hell padre," Anthony said. He then tied a slender necktie around Hernandez's upper right arm, found a prominent vein and injected a lethal dose of the pure heroin into Hernandez's blood stream.

"Tony! Tony! Don't do this!" Hernandez screamed. He quieted down as the drugs took immediate effect. Anthony stepped back as his body began to jerk rapidly and he started foaming at the mouth. The chair toppled over from the force of his movements. His bowels loosened and his body twitched for another thirty seconds and then he was still. Anthony spat on the body and hurried over to the safe that was in the back of the closet. He opened it and removed the stacks of US currency. He took the money to his room and threw it in a bag. He then removed the money he had in his safe and added it to the bag. He grabbed a few more pieces of clothing from the closet and put those in the bag that he had been packing earlier. Anthony grabbed the two bags and headed downstairs. He threw them in the Range Rover and started the vehicle. He then ran back to the house and dumped flammable liquid all over the living room. He lit a match and flicked it behind him as he hurried back to the garage. The flames spread quickly as Anthony drove out of the premises. He heard an explosion as he turned onto the main road. The fire had reached the gas in the kitchen.

When Mayweather had hurriedly left the mansion having realized that Anthony had somehow killed his men, he had driven down

Stony Hill at speeds he hadn't driven at in years. He had eventually stopped at a pub on Constant Spring Road and had a strong shot of white rum to calm his nerves. It took two shots before he was calm enough to analyze the situation. He rubbed the glass as he tried to decide his next move. Garcia would not stop until he killed him. Mayweather borrowed the bartender's phone and placed an anonymous call to 119. Told them he heard a lot of shots being fired on the premises at 4 Thompson Road in Stony Hill. He hoped Anthony would be there when the cops arrived. He then jumped in his truck and headed home. He had to teach his wife a lesson. The day had gone downhill from the moment the bitch had back-talked him.

Terri got home at eight-thirty that night. The house phone rang as she went inside the bedroom. It was Anna. Terri told her that she had just got home and would call her back later. Terri stripped off her clothes and lay on the bed in her underwear. She wondered how come she hadn't yet heard from Anthony. If he didn't call her by the time she had showered and eaten, she would call him. They definitely had to talk. Tonight.

CHAPTER 11

The police and the fire truck arrived at the burning mansion minutes apart. A motorist, on his way home, had noticed the flames and called the Fire Brigade. The house was gutted but the firemen were able to contain the blaze and prevent it from spreading to the rest of the property. The senior detective who was on the scene was shocked when he saw the three dead bodies outside. The one on the porch had been scorched and the face had been practically blown off but the other two close to the poolside were easily recognizable. What the hell were they doing up here? He took out his cell to call Detective Corporal Miller.

Anthony dialed Gavin's number as he made his way to the luxurious hotel.

"Gavin, something serious has happened," Anthony said when Gavin came on the line.

"What's up?" Gavin asked.

"Mayweather has turned on us," Anthony informed him. "He sent a death squad up to the mansion to kill everyone."

"What!" Gavin exclaimed.

"Everyone is dead," Anthony continued, as he turned onto Knutsford Boulevard. "I'm lucky to be alive."

"Shit, Pablo is dead?" Gavin said in disbelief.

"You better believe it...even the women were killed."

"Mayweather must be gone crazy, I mean...why would he do that?" Gavin was in a state of shock.

"I don't know but I intend to find out," Anthony replied as he pulled up at the front of the hotel. "Listen, I'm gonna be staying at the Regal Court until I figure things out. Do not, under any circumstances, tell anyone. I'll be registered under the name Hector Cotto."

"Ok Tony," Gavin responded in a subdued tone.

"Did you place the order for the Hummer?"

"Yeah, it'll be here in another week or so."

"Cool. I'll use the Range Rover until then. I'll call you if I need anything." Anthony hung up the phone and gestured for a porter to get his two bags. He then parked in the parking lot and went inside the lobby.

He registered under the name Hector Cotto using his fake US passport as ID. He rented one of the penthouse suites for a week and headed to his room on the tenth floor, with the porter in tow. The suite was large and luxurious. Definitely worth every penny, Anthony thought as he looked around approvingly. He tipped the porter fifty US dollars and the porter thanked him and told him to just call down and ask for Joel whenever he needed anything. He left and Anthony stripped down and went into the bathroom to take a shower.

Terri arrived at the crime scene ten minutes after she had received the call. She had quickly gotten dressed and as she basically lived only five minutes from Thompson Road, she got there in no time. She exited her car and walked over to where the detective who had notified her was standing. He looked up from his notepad when she approached.

"Hi Detective Miller," he said.

"Hey, Gary," Terri responded. She watched the firefighters fight to put out the last of the blaze. "What have we got here?"

"Well, so far, we have four dead bodies, including three cops -well only two have been positively identified so far, and some spent shells that should be of interest to you." He held out a clear bag that contained eighteen spent shells.

Terri took the bag and peered at it closely. Some of the shells appeared to be from the same make weapon that had been used in three of the previous murders that she was investigating.

"These guys," he said, referring to the dead policemen, "were definitely here on an operation. A black jeep which is owned by Sgt. Brown was found on the premises. The way they were dressed and the weapons they were carrying also indicate that this was a sting operation."

He paused and continued, "What I find strange is that none of the senior officers and neither the Superintendent in charge of this area knew of any sting operation that was supposed to take place here tonight."

"Hmm," Terri murmured thoughtfully. It was rumored that this set of guys were part of a death squad that Mayweather had assembled. It was also rumored that they were mixed up in all kinds of illegal activities. Several complaints had also been filed against Sgt. Brown for excessive use of force.

"I need to know who owns this property urgently," Terri said to the detective. "Have that information on my desk first thing in the morning."

"Yes, Detective Miller," He replied, "Will do."

Terri walked over to the garage. The charred remains of a large SUV and a sports car were in there.

"I also need to know the make of these two vehicles as soon as possible."

The detective nodded and made a note on his pad. Terri told him to accompany her to have a look around the property.

Mayweather got home and parked his truck in the garage. He took his briefcase and went into the house. His wife was seated on the couch watching a local program. She looked up but did not greet him. He ignored her and went into the bedroom. He decided to take a shower before dealing with her. His cell phone rang as he undressed. It was Detective Foster. The detective told him about the scene in Stony Hill and asked him if he knew of any sting operation that was supposed to take place there this evening. Mayweather told him no and instructed him to have a comprehensive report on his desk first thing in the morning. Ten minutes later, clad in a pair of white briefs, he made his way to the living room.

Elaine heard him come to a stop behind the couch in which she was sitting. Her heartbeat accelerated but she continued to look at the TV and did not acknowledge his presence. Mayweather stood behind his wife and looked at her. After a few moments he grabbed a fistful of her hair. Elaine screamed and tried to get up. A hard punch connected to her right ear. She stopped struggling as her head pounded in pain.

"Who the fuck was you talking to like that earlier? Hmm?" Mayweather snarled, as he leaned over her with her hair tightly wound in his fist.

"Claude...why are doing this?" Elaine sobbed.

"You are a poor excuse for a woman much less a wife," Mayweather told her. "Add that to the fact that you start back talk mi now and we have a serious problem."

His cruel words enraged Elaine. She twisted suddenly, ignoring the pain and turned around to face him. She slapped his face as hard as she could.

Mayweather was shocked. This was the first time she had ever attempted to fight back. He released her hair and punched her in the mouth. Elaine squealed and toppled over. She tried to crawl away, as he hopped over the sofa and advanced on her. Elaine was scared for her life. She had never seen him this enraged. She scrambled up and grabbed the vase off the table. He administered a hard punch to her stomach. Elaine howled and doubled over in pain still clutching the vase.

"You ungrateful bitch," Mayweather was saying, "After mi ah provide fi yuh all these years, while you sit down and eat and watch soap opera all day... yuh ah come bright...." Elaine straightened up and hit him over the head with the vase. The vase shattered and left a deep gash on his forehead. She jumped on him, knocking over the small table that had their wedding photos and sank her teeth in his neck. Mayweather screamed and grabbed her right breast which he twisted painfully. Elaine cried out and Mayweather took the opportunity to push her off him. They both scrambled to their feet. Mayweather's neck throbbed from the bite she had inflicted. She noticed that he had an erection. No way you're fucking me tonight Elaine thought to herself and turned and sprinted to the kitchen. Mayweather charged after her in hot pursuit. She grabbed a huge kitchen knife out of the holder on the counter and turned around as Mayweather screeched to a halt.

He smirked at her. "What yuh going to do with that except make me even angrier? Put the knife down bitch!"

"Fuck you Claude, you brute!" Elaine shouted, crying. "If you touch me again I'm going to stab you."

Mayweather lunged at her and Elaine swung the knife, opening a deep gash on his chest. Mayweather stopped in his tracks and stared in disbelief at the cut on his chest. Elaine looked at him defiantly, holding the knife steadily in front of her.

"Mi ago kill yuh rass!" Mayweather snarled and turned to go into the bedroom. Elaine realized he was going for his firearm. She ran after him. Mayweather heard her coming and started to run. He reached the bedroom and opened the draw to take out his revolver. Elaine, running faster than she had ever run in her adult life, jumped on Mayweather as he took the gun out of the draw. The weapon went off and the bullet lodged in the ceiling. Elaine screamed as she struggled with her husband. They rolled on the floor grunting as they crashed into the furniture, knocking stuff over. Mayweather squeezed the trigger again and the bullet lodged into the wall. Elaine got desperate and bit her husband in the face. Mayweather screamed in agony and loosened his grip on the gun. She dug her teeth in his flesh mercilessly and he finally let it go. She grabbed it and rolled off him shakily. Her dress was torn, her face was swollen and she was sweaty and disheveled. Mayweather got off the floor like a man possessed and roared as he charged at his wife.

"Claude stay back!" Elaine shouted as she backed up with the gun pointed at him. He ignored her and kept coming. Elaine closed her eyes and fired two shots. Mayweather toppled over. Elaine sank to the floor. She was in shock. She had just shot her husband.

"Oh god!" Elaine moaned as she let go of the gun and sobbed. The bastard deserved it but she had hoped it would have never come to this. She didn't know how long she sat there crying before she heard sirens approaching the house. The police had arrived. She didn't move. Five minutes later they escorted her from the bedroom in handcuffs and placed her in a squad car. Elaine watched the proceedings from the back of the police car like it was a nightmare that came to life. The yard and house was a bed of activity as the police secured the crime scene. One of the officers had attempted to speak to her but she remained silent.

Terri sped as she hurried to Mayweather's home in Cherry Gardens. She had left Stony Hill as soon as she had gotten the call that the Assistant Commissioner had been killed; presumably by his wife. Terri had instructed the officer in charge not to take Mrs. Mayweather down for processing until she got there. Terri's head was spinning. There had been so much death and chaos over the last couple days. She had never experienced anything like it.

Anthony grinned as he poured champagne all over the girl's body as they sat in the hot tub that was in the bedroom. Earlier, after he had taken a shower, Anthony had ordered room service and called his favourite escort service to send someone over for the night. The girl moaned as Anthony tweaked her nipples and bit her gently on the neck. She protested when Anthony tried to enter her without a condom but shut up quickly when she saw the expression on his face. She spread her legs and prayed he was clean. Five hundred US dollars was good money for a night's work but she liked to protect herself.

Terri arrived at the scene and was met by the lead detective as soon as she exited her car.

"Mi can't believe she kill the Assistant Commissioner," he said to Terri.

"Detective Holness, please pull yourself together and refrain from making such statements at this fetal stage in the investigation," Terri replied sternly.

The detective was not pleased at what she said but he held his tongue. Bitch! He fumed.

"Fill me in on what is known thus far," Terri instructed as she looked over at the squad car in which Elaine Mayweather was seated. She looked lost and distraught. Her mouth was bloody and swollen. Terri listened to the detective and then she went into the house. She looked at Mayweather's bloody body lying in the bedroom. The world is a better place she thought, that woman should be given a medal. She went outside to have a word with Elaine.

Terri opened the door and sat next to her.

"I can only imagine what you're going through. I'll have to take you down to headquarters for questioning. I'll see to it that you get to contact your lawyer so that he can be present when we interview you. After that we'll take pictures documenting the physical evidence and send you to the hospital to get checked out by a doctor. I'll allow him to keep you overnight for observation. Your travel documents will be seized but there'll be no arrest until after the investigation is completed, which I'll personally see dealt with to ensure that it's done in a timely fashion." Terri patted her arm. "This will be over soon and you can move on with your life."

Elaine nodded and told her the name of her attorney. Terri made the call for her and instructed the lawyer to meet them at police headquarters. Terri then told one of the junior officers to take Mrs. Mayweather away and keep her isolated until her lawyer got there. She then went to talk to the press who had just arrived and were buzzing excitedly like bees. This was breaking news.

Anthony took the girl out on the balcony and enjoyed the breathtaking view of the city as he leisurely fucked her from behind. She moaned appreciatively at his prowess. Despite her discomfort at his insistence in not using a condom and his cold demeanor, she thoroughly enjoyed earning the five hundred dollars. He was an exceptionally good lover. Anthony took a swig from the freshly opened bottle of champagne and handed her the bottle. She took a drink and spread her legs wider as he increased his tempo. His mind flashed on Maria and he wondered why the doctor had not yet called him to give him an update on her condition. He would call him in the morning. He hoped she was ok. Anthony slapped her ass cheeks and grunted as he pulled out and erupted on her back.

Gavin was at home in bed with his wife when he got a call at twelve midnight from one of his police contacts informing him that Mayweather was dead. Fatally shot by his wife. Gavin was stunned. So much had happened today. He was a bit relieved that Mayweather was dead. Ever since Anthony had told him what Mayweather had done, he had been wondering if he would turn on him next. God bless Mayweather's wife. Gavin hugged his wife and went back to sleep.

Terri finally got home at one thirty in the morning. She was physically and mentally drained. Elaine Mayweather's statements had almost bought tears to her eyes. She wasn't surprised at what a brute Mayweather had been but it was chilling to hear the details of how he had abused his wife. Terri had allowed her to spend the night at the hospital for observation instead of following procedure and sending her to lock up until she posted bail. The poor woman had been through enough. Terri wearily undressed and took a quick shower, too tired for her usual ritual of unwinding with music and a bubble bath. She fell asleep as her head hit the pillow. Her last thought was that she did not get a chance to speak with Anthony.

CHAPTER 12

Terri was up bright and early at seven the next morning. She had slept well but wished she could've gotten eight hours. She showered and had muffins and coffee for breakfast. Terri slipped on a black, tight fitting pants suit with a white ruffled shirt and hurried out the door. She had a lot to do today.

The information she had requested from Detective Foster was on her desk when she arrived at the office. She opened the envelope and examined the contents. There was a handwritten note stating that the cars in the garage were identified to be a Cadillac Escalade and a BMW 3 Series. Terri felt her excitement rising. There was also a copy of the land title for the premises at Thompson Road. The house had been purchased a little over a year ago. The owner was Pablo Hernandez. The attorney on record was Gavin Wilkinson. Terri grabbed her keys. She was going to throw everything she had at Gavin Wilkinson. He was the key. It was time to bust this case wide open. Terri called Detective Foster on her way out the door.

"Good morning, detective," Terri said. "Good job. I received the information."

"Thank you, Corporal Miller," he replied. That was one of the reasons he respected her so much. She really knew how to make people feel appreciated. He also had a crush on her but kept it buried as he figured that she was way out of his league.

"I need you to go up to the hospital personally to check in on the widow. I'm rushing out to follow up a lead. If things go as planned I might need some back-up, so stand by."

"Will do," Foster replied.

Terri hung up and made her way onto Hope Road. She hoped that Gavin was already at his office. This visit needed to catch him off guard.

Anthony ordered breakfast and went out on the balcony to relax. He called the doctor for an update on Maria.

He answered his mobile on the third ring.

"Hello."

"Doc, it's Anthony Garcia, what is the status on Maria?" Anthony queried, as he looked down on the hustle and bustle of the early morning New Kingston traffic.

Dr. Williams was confused for a moment and then he remembered. That lovely Hispanic woman. "Oh yes, Mr. Garcia," He responded. "She's recovering well. Her...umm... anus was badly torn and there was a little bit of internal bleeding but we performed a minor surgery which was successful in repairing the damage. She needs to stay in the hospital for at least another week."

"Good, good. What time are visiting hours?" Anthony asked.

"Ten to two and then six to eight. I trust the rape was reported to the authorities?"

"Yes, it was," Anthony replied. "Thanks, doc. I'll talk to you some other time."

Anthony ended the call and went back inside. The girl was still under the covers sleeping. Anthony looked at her for a moment. She was really cute and a good lay. Depending on how the day went he might book her again for tonight. Terri crossed his mind as he told the porter to come in. He hadn't gotten a chance to call her back yesterday and she hadn't called him either. Anthony stroked his chin and gestured for the porter to put the food out on the balcony. He decided to wait until she got in touch with him. Anthony nudged the girl awake and told her to come and have some breakfast. He tipped the porter who stole a few glances at the girl as she got up from the bed nude and went to the bathroom.

"Sexy, huh?" Anthony said to him grinning.

"Uhhh...yeah man," the porter agreed and left. What a man cool, he said to himself as he went in the elevator and headed downstairs.

Terri arrived at Gavin Wilkinson's offices on Slipe Road at eight thirty. He owned the entire building. She sat in the car and dialed his office number.

"Good Morning, this is Judge Baker, is Mr. Wilkinson in?" She asked when the receptionist came on the line.

"Good morning, Judge, yes, he is, hold for transfer."

Good he's in. Terri hung up the phone and dialed Foster's number. "Come down to Wilkinson's office on Slipe Road. When you arrive, just park outside and wait. Arrest him as soon as he leaves the building." Terri then exited the car and put on her fashionable black shades and went inside.

She whipped out her ID at the receptionist. "Official police business, I'm going in to see Mr. Wilkinson. Do not, under any circumstances young lady, buzz him on the intercom or I'll arrest you for obstructing a police officer in the line of duty. Understood?"

"Yes, Ma'am." She said nervously, wondering what her boss had done.

With that settled Terri made her way to his office. She opened the door and stepped in. Wilkinson looked up from a file he was reviewing in surprise when Terri entered his office.

"Morning, Gavin," Terri said pleasantly, "and how are you today?"

"Detective, what is the meaning of this intrusion? You can't just barge in here like this!" Wilkinson said angrily.

Terri took the land title out of her pocket and threw it on his desk. "What is your relationship with Pablo Hernandez?"

Wilkinson tried to keep a poker face as he reached for the document. He looked at it. How much did she actually know? Not much or she would've arrested him. He decided to play it cool. "He was a client," Gavin said, shrugging his shoulders dismissively.

"Was? Did he fire you recently or is it because he was killed last night?" Terri asked quickly.

Gavin groaned as he realized his mistake. "No...I meant is."

Terri got up angrily and walked around his desk and grabbed him by his tie. "Listen to me Wilkinson...stop fucking around or I'll have an interrogation squad whisk you away and extract the information I need from you. Too many people have died and this ends today! So how you want to do this?"

"Unhand me detective," he demanded, "You think I'm some punk that you can railroad with idle threats?"

"What are credit cards in your name doing in Anthony Garcia's wallet?" Terri asked quickly, going for broke.

Shit, they got Anthony! Wilkinson thought. How else would she know? Wilkinson panicked. "I don't know what he told you but I wasn't mixed up in any of their activities. I handled a few things for them, all legitimate transactions I might add, that's it detective. Nothing illegal and I can prove it." His mind was churning. If she left here without arresting him he would flee to Europe. Once they really started digging they would uncover all the dummy corporations that he had set up for Hernandez to launder drug money. With the new anti-drugs law being implemented he could do up to thirty years. At his age that's a life sentence. He started to sweat.

Terri released his tie and smoothed his shirt. She went back to sit in the chair in front of his desk. "Ok, start at the very beginning and tell me everything regarding your association with Anthony Garcia and Pablo Hernandez." She folded her hands across her bosom and discreetly pressed the record button on her cell phone. It had the capacity to record for an hour. She would get most if not all of what she needed in that time. She didn't. She listened, fascinated, to Gavin as he told her about Hernandez and Garcia for the next ninety minutes. She could see the holes in his narrative where he omitted certain details in trying to protect himself. Terri felt disgusted. She couldn't believe she had fallen for a big time drug dealer and cold-blooded murderer. Though Gavin could not say for sure, Terri was convinced that Anthony had been the trigger man in at least three murders and was involved in the shootout up by the mansion. All she needed to cement the case was his gun.

When he was through, Terri asked, "Where is Garcia now?"

"He's in a penthouse suite at the Regent Court Hotel, registered under the alias Hector Cotto. He's been there since last night." Oh God please don't let her take me in now...all I need is three hours and I'm off the island, Gavin prayed silently.

"You've been most helpful Gavin," Terri informed him standing up. "I'll need to speak with you later today. Ensure you're available."

Wilkinson was giddy with relief. There really is a God. "Oh, yes, detective," He enthused. "If I'm not in office you can reach me on my cell."

"Good." Terri turned and left. As soon she was out of his office, Gavin got up quickly and removed the painting on the wall. He opened his safe and removed all the money and documents. He stuffed everything in a bag and called a travel agency.

When Terri exited the building, she noticed Foster's unmarked police car parked on the premises. She got in her car and drove out. She called Foster on his cell as she made her way to the Regent Court Hotel. "He should be out any minute now. Arrest him and take him to the Half-Way-Tree lock-up. He's to be charged with money laundering and aiding and abetting known criminals. He's to be placed in a solitary cell. I don't want anything to happen to him before trial. His travel documents are to be seized and his office compounded. I'm heading to the Regent Court Hotel. Bring a plainclothes team and come up to the penthouse suite registered under the name Hector Cotto. Also a grey Range Rover should be in the parking lot. Send someone immediately to keep a close eye on it. Anyone who gets behind the wheel is to be arrested. Got all that?"

"Yes, Corporal," Detective Foster replied. Wilkinson hurriedly exited the building as he came off the phone.

"Let's go," Foster said to the junior detective with him. They hopped out of the car and pulled their firearms.

"Police! Get on the ground!" They shouted, as they approached Wilkinson with their guns trained on him.

Wilkinson's legs felt weak when he heard the shout. He thought he would have gotten away. The bitch had tricked him. He ran to his car and jumped in. The two policemen fired and blew his tires out. They ran up to the car and yanked him out. People in the office building watched the drama unfold through the windows. The police then cuffed him and took him to the unmarked police car. They threw him in the backseat along with the bag that he was carrying and drove to the Half-Way-Tree police station. Detective Foster then called a senior detective and told him to take a team of officers over to Wilkinson's office and confiscate all his files.

Terri was nervous when she pulled into the parking lot of the hotel. She parked, took a deep breath and got out of the car. She touched her firearm as if to reassure herself that it was there and entered the hotel lobby. She went over to one of the three receptionists that were at the front desk. She identified herself and asked to speak with the General Manager urgently. A porter led her to the Manager's office. Terri told her not to panic but there was a strong possibility that a dangerous criminal was staying in the hotel under an assumed name. The Manager, shocked, asked her what she should do. Terri told her not to raise an alarm. Everything was under control. The plan was to surprise him in the room and get him out discreetly without alarming the guests. The Manager nodded with a worried look on her face and checked the name on the computer.

Hector Cotto. Rm 810. "He's in Room 810 on the tenth floor. It's the suite directly facing the elevator." She opened her top drawer and took out a stack of cards. She fished through and handed one to Terri. "The room key," she said nervously. Why did this have to happen on her shift?

"Don't worry, everything will be fine, my back-up will be here shortly," Terri said soothingly. She then got up and went to the elevator.

It was an emotional ninety second ride. Terri was angry at herself for being so stupid. The signs had been there and she had ignored them or made excuses. She should have confronted him from the moment she became suspicious. She was angry with herself for getting caught up and sleeping with him so easily. On the other hand, she had enjoyed being with him immensely. He had stirred something deep in her soul. That, she could not deny. When the elevator reached its destination, she stepped out and stood before Room 810. Terri took a deep breath and cleared her head. Anthony was a dangerous man. She couldn't afford to slip up. Terri pulled her firearm, cocked it, slid the card in the lock and opened the door.

Doctor Williams checked in on Maria after he had finished treating his first batch of patients. He thought she was sleeping but she opened her eyes and looked at him as he stood by her bedside.

"How is my prettiest patient feeling today?" he asked with a smile.

She returned his smile wearily. "Not too bad," she replied softly.

"Your friend called me to check up on you this morning," he informed her, "I think he's going visit you today."

Maria smiled. It would be good to see Tony. He had saved her life.

"Ok, then, I'll see you later," Dr. Williams said. What a woman, he thought as he made his way to the cafeteria. His wife had passed away three years ago and he was lonely. He was a good catch and had no shortage of takers, but he had yet to meet the one. Maria had stirred something in him. He hoped he would get a chance to know her. He wondered what her relationship with Anthony was. The man was young, handsome and obviously well-off, he couldn't compete with that. Well, it makes no sense to speculate, he mused as he looked at the menu on the wall; I'll just ask her.

Terri entered the room holding the gun steadily in front of her. As she closed the door, Anthony and the girl came out of the bathroom laughing. They were both nude and Anthony was hugging her from behind. The girl screamed when she saw Terri holding the gun. Anthony's grey eyes popped open wide in surprise.

"Don't move. Release the girl and both of you put your hands up," Terri instructed, her face an icy mask.

Anthony reacted by putting his arm around the girl's throat and moving swiftly over to the bed, using her as a shield.

Terri realized he was trying to go for his gun but was reluctant to shoot as she didn't want to harm the girl. "Anthony! Stop!" Terri shouted, though she knew he wouldn't. Things were off to a bad start. She had expected him to be alone in the suite.

Anthony grabbed his gun and held it at the girl's head, while still standing behind her. "Put your gun down Terri or she's dead. Do it now!"

"Anthony don't do this," Terri pleaded, "let her go. This is between me and you."

"I'm only going to tell you one more time. Put down your gun," Anthony replied coldly.

"I can't do that Anthony," Terri said. "Be a man. I came here by myself. Let the girl go. Don't tell me the great killer Anthony Garcia is afraid of a little female cop."

Anthony knew that she was trying to mess with his head but her words still rubbed him the wrong way. The girl sobbed in his arms. Fuck it.

He trained his gun on Terri and pushed the girl away. "Grab your shit and get the fuck outta here." She didn't need to be told twice. She hurriedly scooped up her dress, handbag and shoes, and ran to the door. Terri moved aside to let her pass but kept her gun and eyes on Anthony. The girl went out and Terri nudged the door shut with her foot.

They stared at each other silently; their bodies taut with tension. Remarkably, even now, she couldn't help but admire how sexy he was. In another lifetime, he could've really made her happy. Life was really a bitch. The man who had inexplicably captured her heart and tantalized her body was a ruthless killer. This standoff would end badly. She knew there was no way Anthony would allow her to arrest him. Terri felt as if her chest would burst.

Anthony felt excited and disappointed at the same time. The showdown had been inevitable but he hadn't expected it to happen so soon. There she was, looking good enough to eat in her black suit holding a gun at him, her bosom heaving with nervous excitement. He sighed as he felt himself getting erect.

"That punk Gavin just can't keep his mouth shut, huh? I'll shut it for him permanently when I get out of here."

Terri tried to ignore his rapidly growing erection. Unbelievable, Terri thought. "You won't be getting out of here Tony; this is where the buck stops. Your killing days are over."

Anthony chuckled. "Do you really think you can kill me Terri?" he asked softly as he started to walk slowly towards her.

Terri's palms began to sweat. She gripped her firearm tightly and took an involuntary step back. "Tony, please... don't come any closer or I'm going to shoot...back-up is on the way. There is no way out. Please...just surrender."

Anthony kept smiling as he continued to move towards her. "It was good, wasn't it T? But as they say, all good things must come to an end."

They both fired simultaneously.

Detective Foster and a team of four policemen hurriedly entered the lobby. The Manager had instructed the front desk to advise any police officer who came in to go to Room 810. Foster approached the desk and flashed his ID. The receptionist immediately told him the room number without him having to ask.

"Come on!" Foster said and they raced to the elevators. Foster prayed that she was ok.

Terri leaned against the door in pain. Damn, that gun really packs a punch, she thought, grimacing. Her right shoulder where the bullet had entered was hurting really badly. She looked at Anthony who was lying on the floor. He was coughing up blood. Terri walked over and knelt beside him. Anthony looked at Terri as he felt the Grim Reaper approaching. The bullet from her 357 Magnum had ripped his stomach to shreds. The pain was excruciating. He knew he could've killed Terri and shot his way out of the hotel, but he just couldn't bring himself to do it.

"I know you deliberately shot me in the shoulder," she said to him softly.

He grimaced as he looked at her; his intense grey eyes filled with pain and sadness. "How could I kill the only woman I ever loved?"

Terri's eyes filled with tears as she thought how crazy life could be sometimes. She held his hand and he coughed one final time and was still.

Detective Foster kicked the door in and the five cops barged in the room with their guns ready.

He holstered his gun and knelt beside Terri as the others looked around the suite. "Are you ok?"

"Yeah," she replied, "it's just a shoulder wound."

"Well, you're losing blood so we need to get you to the hospital." He helped her up and instructed the other men to secure the crime scene. As he helped her to the elevator Detective Foster wondered what the hell was going on. She obviously wasn't crying because of the wound to her shoulder. And she was holding the dead man's hand when he came in the room. He wouldn't pry though. Whatever had taken place, the important thing was that the murderer was caught.

EPILOGUE

Terri looked out the bedroom window down at the swimming pool. She watched the four young boys as they played water polo. She was at her parents' condo in a gated community in Florida. They traveled to Miami at least six times a year so they had invested in the property two years ago. It had been four weeks since the shooting at the hotel. The bullet had damaged some ligaments in her right shoulder but her arm was expected to regain full strength in a couple of months. The Commissioner of Police had publicly lauded Terri for her bravery and for solving the case. He also promoted her to Assistant Superintendent of Police in charge of Kingston and St. Andrew. It was unprecedented. She was only twenty-seven years old. The promotion was not yet public however, as Terri had told him she needed to take some time off to sort out some personal issues and would discuss it with him when she returned.

So, here she was in Miami on one month's leave of absence. Her mother and Anna had offered to accompany her but she needed to be alone. She was pregnant with Anthony's baby. When she had found out that she was pregnant, she knew the best thing was to go abroad. That way, if she decided to abort it, no one would know. Terri sighed and sipped her juice. If she had the baby, what would she say when it asked for its father? What would her parents say when she suddenly told them she was pregnant and she wasn't married or even engaged to the father? They would flip when she refused to tell them who the father is. If she had the baby she would have to remove herself from frontline duties and get a desk job. She couldn't afford for anything to happen to her. The baby would be an orphan.

Terri felt alone as she grappled with the most important decision of her life since deciding what to major in at university nine years ago.

Maria sipped a glass of wine as she stirred the pasta. She was in Dr. Williams' kitchen at his cozy three-bedroom house in Barbican. He was a Godsend. When he had told her the news of Anthony's death the day after it happened, she had cried for a few days. She had been devastated. She had always thought that she would be with Anthony after getting out of the hospital. She had panicked when she analyzed her situation. She was thirty four years old, in a foreign country illegally and her access to money was gone. Fortunately, when Dr. Williams had approached her and told her that he wanted to have a relationship with her, he hadn't changed his mind when she told him about her past; though it was a slightly watered-down version. She had now been living with him for three weeks. They slept in separate bedrooms and were yet to have sex. Ah, Maria sighed, such an understanding man. Maria hoped he would still be when she spoke to him tonight. She was pregnant. Her period was late and she had taken a pregnancy test. She was positive it was Anthony's.

Elaine Mayweather relaxed on her new leather couch as she watched her favourite soap opera. She was over the shock of killing her husband. His death had been ruled as justifiable homicide. She was also a fairly rich widow. Her husband had bank accounts with vast sums of money that she hadn't known about. She planned to go to the gym, lose some weight and travel the world. The second phase of her life was just beginning and she planned to make damn sure that she enjoyed it to the fullest.

Howard flushed the toilet and looked at his reflection in the mirror as he washed his hands. He couldn't believe it when Mrs. Mayweather had instructed him yesterday to come inside and have a word with her before he started any work around the yard. She had told him that now that she was single and moving on with her life, she was interested in having him in her life intimately, if he was interested. He had showed her just how interested he was right there on the couch.

To his surprise, she was an animal in bed. She had hungrily ravaged his young, firm body. Life was certainly full of surprises. He dried his hands and went to join her on the couch.

Terri felt lighter when she went to bed that night. She had finally made a decision. She would keep the baby. She would have to make a few changes in her life but she was going to have her baby. She dreamt of her baby's father that night.

OTHER TITLES BY THE AUTHOR:

Novels & Anthologies:
The Stud
Erotic Jamaican Tales
More Erotic Jamaican Tales

Compilations:
LMH Official Dictionary Series (Co-authored with M. Henry):
- ❖ LMH Official Dictionary of Popular Jamaican Phrases
- ❖ LMH Official Dictionary of Jamaican Words & Proverbs
- ❖ LMH Official Dictionary of Jamaican Herbs & Medicinal Plants & their uses
- ❖ LMH Official Dictionary of Jamaican History
- ❖ LMH Official Dictionary of Sex Island Style
- ❖ LMH Official Dictionary of Sex Island Style: Volume 2

Breinigsville, PA USA
09 September 2009
223787BV00001B/5/A